BLACKSPACE

Book 1

by Dominique Carthage

DORRANCE PUBLISHING CO
EST. 1920
PITTSBURGH, PENNSYLVANIA 15238

Dorrance Publishing Co
585 Alpha Drive
Pittsburgh, PA 15238
Visit our website at *www.dorrancebookstore.com*

ISBN: 979-8-8852-7111-0
eISBN: 979-8-8852-7838-6

BLACKSPACE

Book 1

ACT 1

Scene 1 (It's Like Las Vegas in New York)

In a city unlike no other lies the tale of power, greed, scandal, corruption, and major crime across the board. A huge metropolitan concrete jungle with vast neon lights that promotes all of your sinful desires and needs. Complete with organized crime and Mafia-like mob bosses. The city called Red Light District was a dark one, literally; the only way to describe the mood is constant rain and cloudy skies.

A packed train was moving through the dense fog of the city in the early morning. A tall, bronze woman in blue jeans and a hoodie sporting African colors stood up to exit the train. Her hair was braided, and her gaze was on her surroundings as she made her way through the subway to the busy Red Light District City streets. The people oblivious to the constant police sirens and occasional gunshots.

She spoke to everyone on her way up to her office, ready to start digging into her brand-new piece for the newspaper. A huge story she has been working on, a possible big lead that could tie a string of murders to a violent narcotics trafficker. Someone knocked on the door and it was the police captain, Commissioner Monroe, who had a cigar in his mouth and a frown on his face. He sat down on the edge of her desk and waited for her to speak, she seemed very nervous.

> M - "Let me explain, Captain, before you start," Mary said, grabbing a file from her bag.

> CM - "Okay, but before you start, I'm not going to keep allowing you to play vigilante out here, your job is to inform the public not play reporter turned private investigator, Mary," Captain Monroe stated, ready to hear her story.

On the opposite side of town, in the slum-filled West District, an apartment complex stood with boarded windows and broken glass strewn across the floor. The scene of a drug deal. Dante was smoking a cigarette and dressed in all black, wearing a black leather jacket, with his hat pulled down low and kicking glass around with his boot. He was blowing smoke out of his nose and had a hand in his leather jacket.

FM - "Why do we always have to come to this rat filled s*** hole, Dante?" Fatman complained, eating a candy bar.

D - "Because this building is condemned and not in the public eye. We need to focus on this deal; we have to deal with the Devino Crime Family this time," Dante said, firing up a cigarette and checking the clip in his .40 caliber pistol.

Two black trench coat-wearing Italians then knocked on the door, which fell down in a big dust cloud, making them cough and laugh. They came in with a duffle bag and dropped it on the floor, showing them the contents of the duffle bag. Dante, in return, presented the drugs and made the drop. The Italians seemed pleased, so they left.

FM - "Easy money; let's get out of this this place," Fatman boasted.

D - "Don't jinx it; we ain't through yet. We got to take this money to our favorite banker, the crazy haired one," Dante said, flicking his cigarette.

FM - "Why do you let this man hold our money? He's shady and just plain weird, bruh," Fatman asked, chewing his candy.

D - "I trust him; he's a straight shooter, and his crazy a** antics help keep things interesting," Dante said.

He heard the sound of footsteps and grabbed his gun and motioned for Fatman to get down. Through a broken chunk of the worn wall, he saw FBI tactical agents in the hall marching towards the room. He motioned for Fatman to climb out the window and climb down the fire escape. Fatman struggled to get out of the window as Dante threw a match into the room on the gasoline that he poured earlier that evening in the abandoned building. He fired a few shots towards the FBI van on the corner as they got in his black 2003 Mustang with the duffle bag. The building was fully ablaze by the time they drove off.

FM - "What the f*** was that? I know they didn't set us up like that," Fatman asked.

D - "They probably didn't, but we will find that out later; we got a few trips to make," Dante said, smoking as his cellphone rang.
He looked at it and answered it.

D - "Hello, yes, Rebeccah, I did not forget. I'm wrapping up some things, and I promise I'll be at your show," Dante said, speaking to his younger sister.

He hung up the phone and sped swiftly and evasively through the West District traffic. He passed all of the banks and jewelry stores only to arrive at the pawn shop that was full of strange and weird items. He and Fatman snuck around to the back door in the alley and went through the back door of the shop. They met up with a crazy-haired, silk robe-wearing Jewish merchant known as Goldstein. He was smoking a joint and listening to rock music as Dante dropped the heavy bag of money on the table.

G - "Alright, stop back in the morning. I'll have some clean, untraceable bills, and remember, I'll have to charge extra for blood-soaked bills. Did anything happen this time?" Goldstein asked, passing his joint.

D- "Yeah, it's a long story for another day, and with that being said, it's been a nice visit. We have to go now." Dante smiled, hitting the joint.

G - "Until next time, my friend," Goldstein said.

Dante dropped Fatman off at his girlfriend's apartment and went to the Hipster Bar to watch his sister perform. Beccah was seventeen and was more tree hugger than hipster. She loved her phone and other technology but prefers not to be tied down to her devices. She was excited to see her big brother, whom she looked up to. She ran up to hug him in the smoke-filled club.

R - "I'm so glad you showed up because Louise Lane wouldn't since she's so busy," Rebeccah said.

She had a red cup that Dante took out of her hand. He took a sip.

D - "Apple juice, good selection. Now, you know Mary's job is very detailing and she normally spends long hours at *The Daily Planet*," Dante joked, checking out the club scene.

R - "That's funny, D. Okay, let me go perform our new song and lunch is on me… well, dinner, because a sister is starved," Beccah said, dancing her way to the back to the stage as music vibrated the wall.

Mary was inside of a burned down warehouse in the Fish Market District. She had a flashlight, camera, and her phone. She had no weapons, except Mace. It was dark and damp in the funky warehouse as she hid from view alongside the walls. She was taking pictures of a woman tied on a table, surrounded by lit candles.

As Mary texted Captain Monroe her location, a hooded man in a black cloak approached the table with the tied-up woman. She was sedated, Mary thought, getting her Mace ready. The cloaked man then pulled out a dagger with a red, dull-colored blade and slowly approached the young girl. All of a sudden, the room started to glow red as if fire was present, and the wind even picked up.

Mary was thinking she was going to a suspected gang hangout to find evidence for her story about the string of violent gang murders. But this was paranormal, making her take a lot of pictures. As the man attempted to stab the woman in the glowing red room, Mary threw a big heavy rock and hit the man in the head with it. She then ran up to him and sprayed him in the face with her Mace. She quickly untied the woman and helped her off of the table, grabbing a tattered brown book just as the police arrived. She was helping the woman as the cloaked man started to give chase. She then saw the captain, who quickly drew his firearm on the man.

CM - "FREEZE! Don't move, or I will shoot!" Captain Monroe yelled. "Get the girl downstairs and quickly get outside."

M - "Okay, Captain," Mary said, not stopping or turning around.

She heard a gunshot on her way outside to the closest cop car in the foggy midnight mist.

M - "What in the world is going on?" Mary asked, out of breath. "What did I just witness that was very spooky?" Mary put the woman in the police car.

More cops came, as well as an ambulance for the victim. The captain found Mary, who just hid the spooky old book from the cops. She was ready to tell the captain what she saw. The captain lit his cigar, giving her the nod to speak.

M - "Alright, this is what I have so far, I got here an hour ago to look for anything on the drug murders, but then I stumbled into this room where I saw this woman tied up on the table," Mary recalled, showing him pictures, after deleting the ones with the book in it. "This man came in with a dagger and was going to do who knows what as the room turned red and becoming windy, I was afraid. I hit the man in the head with a rock and sprayed him with the mase you gave me, untied the young woman, and ran out of there, you got here quick, too," Mary recalled.

CM - "You're headed to the station with me. We need to get a statement from you. I would yell at you about how dangerous this was, but that can wait. I think you may have stumbled across something," Captain Monroe said.

Dante and Rebeccah were at Mary's apartment, which was by the Freedom Journal Tower. It wasn't fancy at all and was located above a restaurant and was very modest, especially for an award-winning journalist.

R - "About damn time. You missed my show, too," Rebeccah said, noticing the tired look on her face.

M - "Language, young lady, and I'm sorry. Dante filmed it for me, so I could watch it, but I saw something incredible, and I even got this weird book. It was crazy," Mary said, pouring herself some wine, clutching the old, tattered, and strange book.

D - "Okay, well, let's hear something. I'm interested. Let me see that book; it looks super old," Dante said.

M - "I don't think you want to touch this book. I saw some witchcraft tonight. Let me show you guys," Mary said, grabbing the camera putting her wine glass down.

She was about to show them when the wind picked up in the living room. Suddenly, her camera fried with smoke coming from it. The book pricked her finger, and she dropped the book and camera. They just looked at each other in shock. Mary carefully picked the book up with tongs and sat it on the counter. Words suddenly appeared on the book: "The Eternal Source of Star children," instead of the symbols.

Mary looked at a strange symbol that appeared on her hand as a tattoo of an "S" on her hand. Mary touched the book again. She had a vision that made her faint and fall. Luckily, Dante caught her and sat her down.

Mary was out for five minutes. She was breathing through her nose, asleep on the couch. She arose, yawning.

M - "It gave me memories of the last owner of this book and—" Mary stopped and grabbed her wine glass and had a few sips.

D - "Is it witchcraft or satanic?" Dante asked, just as shocked as Rebeccah and Mary.

M - "Its origins are from a civilization of beings that exist in a galaxy near this one. What kind of book is it?" Mary asked. "I don't know yet, the memories are faded," Mary said, grabbing a pen and writing in her small pad she kept in her jeans.

R - "So, what you're trying to tell me is that this isn't the only planet with life on it?" Beccah asked. "So, are aliens real?" Mary shrugged and was quiet as they all sat around and thought about it.

M - "We can't tell anyone about this until we figure this out, if we should even let anybody know at all," Mary said, looking at the book.

Scene 2 (A Cult of Mystery)

Mary was in her office in the Freedom Journal Tower. She finished her story on the string of gang murders, a task she now found boring. She did such a good job that the gangs sent her death threats. Mary didn't care at all because of the book. It was sending her faded memories of the previous owner's life, culture, and other visions, as well. It could be a historic moment if she told what she knew about the book. She chose to keep it a secret.

What if the idea that another form of intelligent life existing in the form of something that can't be imagined or comprehended be reality? Religious organizations would fall, and she feared that would be the fall of humanity. She made Dante and Rebeccah promise to share the burden of knowing that answer with her.

Her boss walked into her office, the very hands-on CEO Lindsey Townsend. She shook her hand and sat down in her small office.

> L - "It goes without saying, you are a very bright young woman and you're going to be big soon, so let's start now," Lindsey said, the red-haired woman with sharp green eyes sat confidently. "I have a story for you."

> M - "Thanks for the kind words. What's the story, boss?" Mary asked, kind of nervous of what she might say.

> L - "I want information on the StarGaze Society and their ultimate goals, I have reason to believe they are a terrorist organization," Lindsey said, her fingers locked, resting upon her crossed knees.

> M - "If they are a terror cell, then why do you want me instead of calling the FBI?" Mary asked. "I'm just a journalist, not a detective as Captain Monroe tells me every other week," Mary stated.

> L - "Wow, the captain sure has left an impression on you. You are my best reporter, and this story has your name on it,

investigative reporting and I need this group exposed." Lindsey leaned forward in her business suit.

M - "I know you mean well, boss lady, but believe me, people shouldn't know things they may not be ready for," Mary said.

Mary agreed to take on the StarGaze Society as her next big piece, and she also would have her first chance to attend a popular ball for politicians and the Red-Light District officials in a ballroom. The men were in tuxedos and women in gowns and beautiful dresses. It was $10,000 a plate for the fundraiser, and Mary was shocked when she saw Dante. Her brother was in a tuxedo, eating cheese and drinking champagne. So, she quickly approached him in her high heels and conservative dress.

M - "What are you doing here?" Mary asked, softly and quietly.

D - "I had a strong feeling that you'd be here working on some kind of story, so I'm here to observe. I keep having dreams about that book," Dante declared nonchalantly, socializing with the stars, lighting a cigar.

M - "We'll talk later. For now, let's just be cool and play the room," Mary said, smiling and drinking her champagne. She was surprised at how many of them were fans of her work.

They interacted with all of the guests, and Mary felt a strong presence in the room by a man wearing an all-black suit. He was a tall man and had a gothic vibe to him. Mary introduced herself to the man.

M - "Hello, I'm Mary Dawson—" Mary was politely cut off by the man.

The man in the black suit had a ring with a purple stone in the center. Mary recognized the ring as one belonging to StarGaze members. She got a good look at him.

D - "I know exactly who you are... the *Freedom Journal's* brave, courageous, and danger-loving investigative reporter. Call me Dio. And that's your brother, Dante, who has a bad boy side, if you will," Dio said.

M - "Okay, you've really done your research. I have a question," Mary asked. "What does the StarGaze Society have to do with a political fundraiser?" Mary asked, now on alert.

D - "The same reason as you... to mingle and rub shoulders," Dio answered, charmingly. "I think we should talk for a brief moment. Tell your brother to stay here and you follow me," Dio instructed.

Mary followed his instructions and told Dante to continue to party and let her talk to the man. She followed Dio outside of the ballroom to the hallway. As Mary opened the door, she found herself in a room that wasn't there before. It was a plain room, with plain white walls and a dirt floor. The floor was mostly dirt with patches of grass. Mary looked down at the symbol on her hand as it glowed red.

She stepped into the room with a puzzled look on her face. There were two chairs in the small room on the dirt floor. Dio motioned for her to sit down. She did, expecting a trick or something bad to happen, but nothing happened as Dio sat down, as well.

M - "Where are we? I thought a hallway was behind those doors I came in through. What is this?" Mary asked, visibly confused.

D - "Since recorded history man has wondered, how did we get here, does God exist, is there life in the vast black space all around us?" Dio asked, his hands moving as he talks. "So, our StarGaze community was created to find answers in ancient text, as well as modern science. There is so much for us to learn, and we've made discoveries in ancient civilizations that wanted us to expand on their knowledge, but humanity failed to pick up the ball, so insert the StarGaze Society," Dio stated.

M - "Why are you trusting me with this? Aren't you afraid I'd blow your cover? I mean, you're a part of a mysterious cult?" Mary asked. "I'm a reporter and journalist, after all."

D - "We both know that mankind isn't ready for this kind of reality change, but you are, don't you remember your parents?" Dio smiled. "Your bloodline is special; your family is that of extreme importance."

M - "How did my parents die? Who are they?" Mary asked. She was intrigued.

D - "Your parents are—" Dio stopped. "This is our first-time meeting, so I'll let you ask three questions, then you'll have to make a decision of grave significance," Dio proposed.

M - "Have you been influenced or contacted by anything not from this planet?" Mary asked. Dio smiled.

D - "Influenced, yes. I personally have not been contacted by any E.T.s, but I have interacted with some of their technology," Dio said.

M - "Are you using alien tech to create this room?" Mary asked.

D - "I am using such technology. How it operates?" Dio asked. "I don't know yet." Dio grinned confidently.

M - "Where are my parents?" Mary demanded. She was sweating and felt as if she was having a panic attack.

D - "That'll take the fun out of this, but your parents are a great mystery. Only the Grand One can answer that question and for you to know; you'll have to join the StarGaze Society," Dio offered. "My disciples had a book that we need back, and I've noticed the symbol on your hand is the same that appears on the book and other technology," Dio said.

M - "So, are you trying to tell me that I may able to open and decipher the strange language?" Mary asked, she wiped the sweat from her forehead. "Okay, I join your Society, how do I know you will not kill me when you're done and get what you want? I don't want to be tied up on a table," Mary asked, cautiously.

D - "I will personally make sure that nothing happens to you and yes, we were going to sacrifice the woman you found, but that is not for us to discuss. It is you that is the key to this fantastic puzzle," Dio pleaded.

The next day, Mary was in a cab on her way to the StarGaze Temple. It was a chilly, gray morning and the sound of police sirens and people talking and yelling in the sprawling city did not affect her. She was very focused on the Temple because it was a very controversial and mysterious place, closed to the public. Her past attempts to gain entry inside failed terribly, resulting in the canning of one of her stories. But now that she knows strange visitors visited this planet and she can interact with the alien book, the cult would not try to kill her.

She got out of the cab and made her way to the steps of the large, church-like structure, adorned with stain glass windows, that were pretty in a dark way. She brought the book with her in a small briefcase, with a lock on it, to protect it from getting into the wrong hands. As she made her way up to the stairs ready to enter, the huge wooden doors suddenly opened. Her small symbol started to glow red on her hand.

She had a vision of Dio in deep meditation with a small blue globe in his hands. She opened her eyes and Dio was standing in front of her. She now believes that the small orb was an alien artifact he uses to defy physics. She chose to remain calm and tried not to reveal how much she might know. She has a feeling that Dio has the ability to access her mind with the orb. He then made the cantaloupe-sized glowing red orb shrink into a small gem that could fit atop his ring.

She shook his hand and Dio even reassuringly patted her on the back.

> D - "I see you are excited about our journey to the stars, Miss Mary. I feel the same way, as well. Welcome to our beloved Temple." Dio invited her in, opening the doors with a wave of the hand.

> M - "Thank you, I am excited and nervous as hell," Mary said, she walked inside of the grand and mysterious building.

Dio, dressed in his red StarGaze robe, led Mary inside of the Grand Temple. The heavy doors closed behind them.

Scene 3 (Too Rebellious)

Rebeccah was at her school, the School of Performing Arts, or SOPA for short. She has good grades, but the sudden revelation of alien life made the seventeen-year-old question her entire life. She became distant from her friends and bandmates because she couldn't tell them what she was really thinking. She looked up to her sister, so she didn't want to let the information slip into the wrong hands. The three siblings collectively have no memories of their parents or even certain parts of their lives. As far as they know, the last ten years is all they have recollection of.

Beccah faked having the flu in order to get sent home. So, she called Dante, who had Fatman with him in his black 2003 Mustang. They picked her up and he had the talk with her about being secretive, as he swiftly sped through traffic.

D - "I know you are not sick. But you are going home and you're going to wait there in that building until we get back," Dante Commanded her.

R - "No, I'm not. I'm afraid to be alone. I need company and Fatman owes me a game of spades, and I'm hungry. Plus, you promised me we'll hang out today," Beccah pleaded, sitting in the backseat.

D - "We were supposed to hang out after you got out of school, but you left early, and we have adult business to handle, and I don't want you around that. You're too young, and what I do is dangerous and very risky," Dante said, as Fatman chewed a Snickers bar.

R - "I know exactly what you do and so does Mary. I promise not to tell anybody. I can help; look at what I got," Rebeccah said, pulling a small revolver from her Hello Kitty bag.

D - "Oh my God, Rebeccah, where did you get that? Better question: Why do you have a gun? You're a kid," Dante asked. Fatman laughed as she put the gun back in her bag.

R - "I need protection. Plus, the guy I bought it from showed me how to load it and how to use it," Rebeccah calmly answered.

Dante still took her to their apartment they share with Mary above the Korean restaurant and took her gun from her, as well. Rebeccah and Dante sat on the couch and Dante rubbed her shoulder, exhaling deeply. They been through a lot over the past couple of days and he could understand her fear.

D - "I know all this is scary and hard to believe but, that's why we are the ones chosen for this and we need to be calm as to not draw attention to ourselves. Did you have any more weapons while we're here?" Dante asked, looking in her school bag.

R - "I'm not giving you all of my weapons. I'm a young lady in the Red-Light District. I have to protect myself from humans and whatever else is out there," Rebeccah said.

D - "You're right about that, but I don't want you to turn into a gun-slinging cowgirl. Now, if you give me two hours, I'll promise to come back here ASAP. We'll talk to Mary to see what she wants," Dante said.

Dante made his way downstairs to the Mustang parked in front of the building, where Fatman was smoking and trying to flirt with women as they walked by.

They got in the black armored sports car and drove to the Diamond District to meet up with Goldstein at the jewelry store. They went to the back door in the alley and Goldstein came to the door in a silk robe and let them in. They went to the back room and sat down in his office. Goldstein sat down after handing them brown paper bags.

FM - "So, tell us the good news, Goldstein," Fatman asked, looking inside of the brown bag containing cash.

G - "Well, the good news is that rash of yours is curable," Goldstein joked, making Dante laugh, as well. "No, but seriously, there is bad news. The FBI raid from the other night was for you two. You are being targeted by the Drug Task Force," Goldstein informed them.

D - "What is the good news then, sir?" Dante asked, nonchalantly.

G - "The good news is that Captain Monroe came and visited me. Apparently, I'm a part of the conspiracy, too. But he says he'll help us if we help him," Goldstein said. "He wants the briefcase containing a mysterious object. The thing is, the Devino Crime Family has possession of the briefcase, and that's where you two come in," Goldstein said.

D - "Call him and tell him we'll do it," Dante said as he and Fatman left.

They got in the car, and Rebeccah scared them both as she sat up in the backseat and laughed. They tried to play it off, but she startled them.

D- "I thought I politely asked you to stay at home and wait for me there and to not move?" Dante asked, surprised to see her.

FM - "Yeah, you almost gave me a heart attack, Beccah," Fatman said.

R - "I'm sorry, but I just can't be alone right now, and you took my gun from me," Beccah said.

F - "How did you even find us?" Fatman asked, wiping his forehead.

R - "I hid in the trunk," Rebeccah simply said.

Dante thought about how tough Beccah was and all the things she was exposed to over the past years. She was there when he got shot and even help stitch him up. She once stabbed a mugger trying to rob her and worse, she only stabbed him twice, but she did stay there to help him until medical help arrived. Even though she was seventeen, she could handle the worst situations, which made him proud.

D - "Okay, we are being targeted by the Drug Task Force, me and Fatman, if we can get a suitcase for the captain, he'll look out for us, and I'm going to use this as a way to get out of the game for good," Dante said.

FM - "You're my brother from another, I'm down with whatever," Fatman said, dapping him up.

R - "And me, too. I can help. "Rebeccah interjected.

Scene 4 (Catwoman or Girl)

Dante, Fatman and Rebeccah were all dressed in black and ready to roll. They were at the drug safehouse that was like a hideout, somewhere off the grid in the Fish Market District. Dante was on a satellite phone, which was big by normal standards. He was talking to an associate when he noticed Rebeccah's skullcap and pointed out the cat ears on it, looking foolish.

> D - "No, change hats. You're not Catwoman or girl or whatever," Dante said, with the phone to his ear. "Put your beret back on, it makes you look a little older. You look older if you squint."

She listened to him and put her purple beret on, and she still didn't have her gun, so she pouted. Dante decided to treat her like an adult and give her back her gun. He showed her how to aim and reload the gun, which she was familiar with already.

> D - "Never shoot someone in the back, look them in the eyes and only let that be in dire situations, because sometimes and I hate to admit it, but running away and not shooting is the best choice," Dante said, grabbing a shotgun, an automatic-combat one.

They all gathered around a table that had a few printouts of the building they were staking out. Dante was very ready and focused on the mission, he had military training in his past but couldn't remember that part of his life for some reason. He was the first sibling to tie the alien story with their memory loss and no recollection of their parents. He knew a conspiracy like this has layers and he would have to be patient. He felt ready for the challenge and the conventional way won't cut it.

> D - "Okay, the plan is to use non-lethal force on the Devino crime boss and his security detail. We have intel that he has his family with him," Dante said. "We have an ambush set up, do not use our real names, Fatman, you're Whale, I'm

Point, and Rebeccah you're Cat Girl, we are tranquilizing
the security detail first, tie the wife and kids up," Dante instructed everyone in the safehouse.

They then left to get in the armored GMC SUV, compliments of Captain
Monroe. Dante drove them to the ambush spot in New Brington. Dante had
this strange feeling that he would have to get Rebeccah in fighting shape as
she would be a key piece to the puzzle. She would have to learn how to be
more tactical and smart. They arrived at their destination. Dante told them to
get their weapons ready and gave them hand signals so they would move as a
unit.

The trio were in the Italian Mob-controlled city of New Brington, away from
the affluent suburbs. They parked on the opposite side of the road, far away
from the ambush zone. He got on his phone, dialed some numbers and the
plan was underway. Dante gave them the relax signal. It was night time and
they used the darkness to their advantage. They got out of the SUV swiftly
and quietly. Three allies were already there in FBI-like fatigues and face
shields, Dante signaled to lift their rubber bullet guns.

One of the FBI agents swung a battering ram to knock the door down. On the
roof a team of three agents stormed through the windows and caught the
family off guard and the mob goons were shot with rubber bullets and quickly
subdued. Dante smiled as Rebeccah shot her gun.

They tied everyone up and the family was brought downstairs at gunpoint with
their hands up. The mob boss could tell Beccah was a young girl, even though
she tried to conceal her identity.

MB - "Whoever you are, I will find out and I will kill you
and the girl, too," the mob boss yelled, his face turning red.

Dante shot him with a buckshot of rubber bullets from his shotgun that sent
him flying across the floor. His wife and kids were terrified, screaming very
loudly. Dante cocked his shotgun, sending the empty shell flying as he walked
over to the crime boss, pointing the shotgun at him, in front of his terrified
family.

D - "I came for a briefcase that you have. I need it," Dante
said, very seriously.

His wife stood in front of Dante's shotgun very boldly. She had her hands tied behind her back as Dante looked at her.

R - "Everyone lower your weapons now," Rebeccah ordered, and they listened.

MB - "We don't want any trouble. If you want money, I'll give whatever you want, just don't harm my family. I'm who you are dealing with, not them," the mob boss said. Rebeccah put her gun up.

R - "We'll take $50,000 in cash, as well as that briefcase, and we don't have all day, sir," Rebeccah said. She was calm and changed her voice and accent to a southerner. "Put the money in your wife's Gucci purse, and you have ten minutes," Rebeccah demanded.

MB - "That briefcase contains something dangerous. Something out of this world, I won't have to kill you; it will, be ready," the mob boss said.

D - "What exactly is in this briefcase?" Dante asked.

MB - "Only the chosen can gaze upon the object. I don't know what it is, but it killed two of my men by touching it alone. Don't let it get into the wrong hands," the mob boss pleaded to Dante, who had an agent carry his shotgun to the SUV, he stood there believing the man.

Inside of the GMC SUV, Dante kept his team from celebrating. He knew the object was dangerous, but for the time being, they prepared for the vehicle exchange.

FM - "You did good, Beccah. You held your own out there. But why ask for $50K?" Fatman asked.

R - "Thanks. I did all of that to prove to y'all that I'm built for this, it felt natural, like I've done it before," Rebeccah said.

D - "Don't get too gangster, Cat Girl; we've got other things to worry about," Dante stated.

FM - "Aye, D. I don't know if this is anytime to say this, but I have to," Fatman said. "But I really need to have a serious conversation with the both of you."

D - "Let's go to the vehicle and change our clothes, then once we get back to the safehouse, we'll talk. Remember we are being watched and listened to," Dante said.

They arrived at the abandoned train station on the outskirts of New Brington. They had their clothes to change into with them and they changed on the spot. Burning the old clothes and shoes, getting into the black Mustang, leaving the burning SUV behind as they drove off.

Dante went to a upscale car restoration garage in the Diamond District. He already called ahead to let them know he was coming. He parked the car in the garage and a young Asian man came up to him and shook his hand. He wasn't dressed like the other mechanics, but more like a hipster.

G - "Dude, you just brought the Beast in," Gun said.

D - "I know, but I've been trailed by the FBI, it may be bugged. I know you specialize in that. Check the Beast for me?" Dante asked.

G - "Okay, bro, I'll check it out for you. What's up, Beccah? She in on this?" Gun asked, whispering the last part.

R - "Yes, I am and I'm not a baby, either so you can talk straight in front of me, Gun. I'm a part of the team now," Rebeccah boldly said.

G - "Alright, give me an hour or so. You guys can wait up on the upper level on the patio. I'll send my sister up when I'm done," Gun said.

They went on top of the building and sat around in the chairs. Fatman gave Dante the look, indicating the time to tell him what was going on was now.

FM - "I wanna know what's going on with y'all; you guys been acting weird lately?" Fatman asked.

D - "Well, we aren't supposed to tell anyone, but my sister Mary found a book that was created on another planet by intelligent beings. We are to believe that the object in the briefcase is also alien," Dante said, calmly and slowly to him. "We have to unravel this."

FM - "You mean to tell me that you have access to interplanetary artifacts? No way. I always had a feeling we weren't alone in the universe. Out of all our great scientists and astronomers... Why do we know, and they don't?" Fatman asked.

Scene 5 (StarGaze Nebula)

Dio and Mary walked through the temple that was grand, illustrious, and full of gold framed pictures of cult members of importance. The inside alter was located deep underground. Mary noticed they were traveling deep underground via elevator. The walls and floor were made out of colorful blue marble and highly decorated with candles that instantly lit as they walked by them.

Her last memory of her life was her graduation from college and eventually starting at the *Freedom Journal*. So, all of her focus was into making a detailed list of everything she saw. She knew Dio was just an underboss, she wanted to see the Grand One, who had access to more alien tech.

The Grand Alter of the Stargaze Society was very big and had a high ceiling that was gold, with candles fixed in a chandelier. That was at least a two hundred feet in the air and the walls were made out of dungeon-style large bricks. Mary was in awe of the room's dark and mysterious architecture, dark colored bricks and tiles, with dark purple tapestry. In the center was a huge alter, shaped like a pyramid, with steps that led thirty feet in the air.

> D - "From the time man walked on the earth and looked at the stars in the sky, the spark of curiosity was there," Dio said, holding the globe that glowed blue. "How did we get here, who created us, what are the stars and planets relationship to our planet, does God exist?" Dio asked, he extended the globe for her to touch, and she did, trusting him.

She touched the globe, and they were suddenly transported to a dense tropical jungle, crawling with various animals and insects. They moved through the vegetation and shrubbery as if it were a hologram and it was. They found a group of hairy, ape-like hominids smashing rocks and beating their chests in celebration as they made a spear point. Mary noticed a bright light shoot through the dense vegetation and two of the hairy, ape-like creatures instantly vanished.

Mary's jaw dropped and eyes bulged in disbelief as she witnessed what appeared to be a pre-historic alien abduction.

> D - "We know from the teachings and visions of the Grand Master that we were not only visited by very technological

advanced beings, but they manipulated the DNA of our ancestors," Dio explained, extending the globe, letting her touch it again. This time they were in ancient Egypt (Kemet) witnessing the Pyramid's construction. "The question of whom or what interfered with our ancestor's natural evolution, skipping millions of years evolution is one of our greatest missions of the Temple. We don't know enough; the bigger picture is not yet visible. But I stand corrected because you are the key," Dio said, extending the globe again. She looked once more at the huge aqua duct system the Egyptians used to move mega-ton blocks of cut stone. That was another human mystery that modern people pondered.

They used the aqua duct and reservoir system to float the mega stone blocks. There were a lot of people that worked in union. Mary was so intrigued that she had a huge smile on her face and Dio let her have this moment, because he did the same when it was him in the learning position. He extended the globe once again and she touched it and they were back in her bedroom. She was tired so Dio helped her sit down.

M- "Why am I so tired, and why are we here, Dio?" Mary yawned, clutching the book against her chest.

D - "Because uncovering the truth will do that to a person, after a week you won't be able to come back home for quite some time. The temple will be your temporary home. Now rest and keep this our secret for the time being my dear. And I want you to know you're special to our mission; you're the key to the missing chunk of history," Dio said.

M – "When you get the answers, what then?" Mary yawned deeply, he could barely understand her, so he made her get under her blanket. He kissed her forehead.

He held the blue orb and vanished from the room just as Rebeccah and Dante came in. Rebeccah came and climbed under the blanket with her big sister and laid by her side.

R - "We had a long day. It was crazy, sis," Beccah said. "We found that there are more alien artifacts than that book you have. We have one in a briefcase that we stole from a mob boss, but we have to give it to the captain," Rebeccah said, telling her everything.

M - "Yes, I know more exists, listen Dante, I need you to take good care of Rebeccah. I need you to listen to your big brother and stay safe," Mary said softly. "I'm going to be working alongside the High Priest, Dio, from the StarGaze Society," Mary said. "He says I'm the only one that can access and use the alien tech. This stuff should not be in public, I'll call the captain in the morning," Mary said, laying down comfortably.

They left Mary alone to sleep and her dreams were visions of ancient cultures interacting with E.T.s.

ZZZZZZZZZZZZZZZZZZZZZZZ....

She was awoken by her symbol pulsating, feeling like an ant bite. She saw the book open by itself, and she quickly jumped up and ran to the book and touched it's old, yellowed, and tattered pages. She felt a little shock but didn't stop touching it. Trying to read the complex alien language. Mary then passed out and fell to the ground. In her unconscious state, she saw an older woman who looked like an older Rebeccah.

? - "My dear Mary, you've grown up a lot and I see you have started your journey to the stars," the mysterious woman said, reassuringly. "It will be extremely frightening and difficult at first, but you'll understand this text very clearly once you've obtained the Terminal. The language is theirs; it has to be translated, you are from a bloodline of humans that they've allowed to fully understand," the woman said. "Take this very slowly and get used to the idea of life existing on faraway planets. Earth is not that special once you really look at it."

M - "What happened to our memories? Why can't I remember our parents or anything? Are you my mother? Are
you dead, what's your name?" Mary asked.

? - "You are an investigative journalist; you will put the picture together better than I ever could have. You're really
smart and adventurous; come find me when you're ready,"
the woman said.

Mary awoken and wrote down everything in her journal by the bed. She had
to take a pill that she got from Dante to help with her nerves. She told him
what she saw, how she believes that the vision was more than just a vision and
that their parents could be alive on another planet or in space, something out
of their comprehension.

Rebeccah came in Mary's room and sat down on her bed, giving her a tired,
early morning smile.

M - "Good morning. Rebeccah, listen, I need you to go to
school and at least try to play normal. I need you to do that
for me," Mary said, taking advantage of her time. Dante sat
on the dresser.

D - "I can respect your wishes, Mary, you're the boss and all.
But I can't sit still; we have leads that can uncover this huge
conspiracy. We all play a part, I do agree. For the sake of
mental health reasons, Beccah, you should continue to go to
school and play with your band," Dante said, rolling a blunt.

R - "Okay, I'll pretend to be a normal teenager. But I want…
no, I demand to be included in the loop," Rebeccah demanded. She was smaller than her siblings, who towered over
her. "I want access to my weapons."

M - "We'll include you, but we need to be one. I got to admit,
there will be things to happen to me and I won't be able to
tell you guys," Mary said.

Scene 6 (The Pet Monkeys Live)

A few hours later that morning, Rebeccah got up to cook breakfast for her siblings before school. After she was finished, she went to wake Mary and Dante up from their nap because they all were up earlier that morning talking. They all sat around the small table, eating their food, and talking about their upcoming day. Trying to make it a normal breakfast.

> R - "I thought about this all-last night; I kinda want to go to school badly now," Rebeccah said. "I need a distraction from this alien conspiracy," Beccah said, shoveling food into her mouth.

> D- "Good, because you being a kid with this info, there may be a time in the future where you might have to save the school from aliens, just like the movies," Dante joked.

> M - "Dante, stop trying to scare her; now isn't the time," Mary said.

> D - "I'm not trying to scare her. These things happen in the movies, and this feels like a movie. We all have roles to play," Dante said, eating bacon.

They then got ready for their day, they let Beccah get ready first in the bathroom, since she had to be at school on time. She had on her blue shirt and brown khakis; her hair was a huge afro that moved when she moved.

> M - "You know, I can braid really well. I mean, look at mine and this is with no mirror," Mary said, buttoning up her shirt as Dante used the bathroom next.

> R - "I know you're really good at braiding. I just love this afro; it's so majestic and royal," Rebeccah said. "Like Dante said earlier, this feels like a movie and how cool is it that the

main characters are Black and proud," Rebeccah said, using her big pick to puff out her huge afro.

Just then the doorbell rang. Mary notice Beccah reach for her waist.

M - "Coming, hold on," Mary shouted. "Do you have a gun, young lady?" she asked in her motherly tone.

R - "Yes, I have a gun. It's a small .380 revolver, and I'm trained on how to use it," Rebeccah replied.

M - "Don't take that thing to school. I thought that switch blade was enough, now a gun. Well, since we are going through this strange time, I'll look the other way," Mary said, knowing her kid sister was accurate with it.

They went to the living room to find Trixie and Rickey sitting on the couch. She ran to them hugged them both, the drummer and bassist to her metal band. They were Black, as well, and very proud to be. Trixie was eighteen and was a tall, dread-headed light skin girl with freckles and a couple tattoos. She was a free spirit and didn't care how people perceived her.

Scene 7 (Social Distancing)

Trixie and Rebeccah were classmates at the Red-Light District School of the Performance Arts. Beccah loved the school, which had a state-of-the-art library, computer lab, research facility, and talented students she looked up to. She took pride in her grades and performance as she sat in her classes. She realized that keeping her school work up would benefit her. She could be a heroine like Supergirl or Catwoman, where her alter ego had a life of its own.

Trixie was extremely smart and always talked about astrophysics and the planets. She told Beccah many times that she did believe in life being formed and existing off the planet. Rebeccah called her to the theatre while no one was there in the later part of the day, as they were about to leave the school to go home.

Rebeccah took this very seriously as they sat in the empty theatre. Beccah rubbed Trixie's shoulder.

T - "Okay, why are we in an empty theatre?" Trixie asked. "What crazy s*** do you have to tell me? If it requires this much privacy, are you coming out of the closet?" Trixie asked, seriously.

R - "What? No, my sister came across a book that has alien origins. Ever since we found that book, things have been crazy, and the cray-cray part is that there is more alien artifacts other than the book," Rebeccah explained.

T - "Okay then, if they are aliens, why would they leave a book behind, a simple book?" Trixie asked.

R - "The book maybe was given to us during a time when humans only way of receiving knowledge was for it to be written using symbols. We can't read it, though," Rebeccah said. "I know this sounds crazy, but promise me you won't tell Rickey about this or anyone?" Rebeccah asked.

T - "Okay, I won't tell anybody, and I strangely believe you, but this is amazing. If you can prove it, this gives me some-thing to worry about besides our home situation, we're so screwed." Trixie exhaled; her head hung low.

R - "Don't worry about money. I got that covered. Like I said, this alien deal is the real deal and now that you know, you're a part of the mission. I really need you right now, we will continue to go to school and rock, but we need to unravel this mystery with Dante and Mary," Rebeccah said.

T - "Okay, I'm game, but please don't be on drugs because you sound really zooted right now. I love you still," Trixie said, kissing Beccah's cheek.

R - "I'm not on drugs, Trixie." Rebeccah giggled. "But I am serious; we are going on an adventure, and I'm going to need my bestie with me."

Rebeccah and Trixie were in the principal's office the next morning. Rebeccah took the opportunity to look on the principal's desk, while she was out for a minute. She had a *Freedom Journal* newspaper on her desk with Mary's latest article. Trixie didn't like her snooping, so she whispered her name.

R - "You're gonna have to start scanning your surroundings and everywhere you go for clues and things we can use. As cool as discovering aliens is, we have to be detectives like Mary, to find clues that lead us to our next adventure. Now look on her desk and tell me about what you see," Rebeccah said.

Trixie looked on the desk and saw Mary's article and a cut out article about a mysterious object the captain found and is holding for observations. Trixie then knew that Rebeccah was really on to something. The principal, Mrs. Monroe, came in and sat down at her desk. She was a very firm, strict disci-plinary. But her efforts to reach out to the students was met with a very positive response. The strict principal had a sense of humor.

T - "Are we in trouble? Because we told them to not shoot those fireworks at the football game, it wasn't a good idea," Trixie nervously said.

MM - "That's not why you're here. You two are here because we have a dance coming up and I thought about your Band's proposal to perform," the principal said, folding the paper on her desk. She had a monitor with a camera system that allowed her to see all of the big school.

R - "So, we can perform a whole set, then?" Rebeccah asked, getting excited, sitting on the edge of her seat.

MM - "Don't get too excited; it's not a concert, just three of your songs and no profanity. Keep your clothes on this time and no talk of drug usage," Mrs. Monroe said, behind her oak desk.

T - "Deal, Mrs. Monroe, and how did you like the CD we gave you to listen to?" Trixie asked.

MM - "I think you girls are extremely good. I loved it; I'm playing it in my car now. I'm a fan, but I'm still your principal, so tone the dirty lyrics down; you really don't need them," Mrs. Monroe said, and they both nodded in agreement.

R - "Yes, ma'am, thank you. We won't let you down, and I promise Trixie will keep her clothes on while on stage." Rebeccah giggled.

They left the SOPA on the bus and Trixie was looking out of the window quietly with a sad look. Rebeccah reached over and rubbed her shoulder, and they both sat quietly on the thirty-minute ride to their bus stop. They walked the packed streets after hopping off the bus, arms locked. The two of them kept walking until they got to the Pearl Garden Restaurant. The owner was a Korean man, Xi. Xi ran the store and apartments above with his family.

X - "Hello, pet monkeys," Xi said, jokingly. "I'm just kidding. Rebeccah, please don't stab me." Xi laughed.

R - "Ha-ha, very funny, Xi, very funny," Rebeccah said, as she and Trixie sat down at a table. "Has my brother come by?" Beccah asked.

X - "Yes, and he left you a note," Xi said, with his proper voice.

R - "Okay, can you get two salads for us and read that note to me? I like the sound of your voice," Rebeccah asked.

Xi yelled at his son, who quickly got two fresh salads and the note.

X - "Okay, the note says: Me and Fatman have grown men sh** to do. I would tell you to sit in the crib, but you're stubborn as hell. So, please do your thing. Just be safe out there. I'll call you later," Xi said in his royal accent.

Rebeccah got up and gave him a hug to show her appreciation. They then ate. Beccah wanted Trixie to be ready to run a lot of errands in a quick amount of time. Trixie was ready as she rolled a joint on the table in the busy restaurant. Beccah tipped after they ate, which was rare.

They made it to the apartment and Rebeccah led Trixie to her bedroom, locking the door behind them. She made Trixie sit down on the bed.

R - "Okay, this is just the start, but like I said, I got you. Your money problems are over Trixie," Rebeccah said.

She then dumped a Gucci purse over on her lap with $50,000 wrapped in increments of $1K stacks. Trixie screamed as she grabbed one of the stacks of cash and looked at Beccah, then dropped the stack.

T - "So, the alien stuff is real. You really were dead ass. I mean I trust you and all, but you made a lot of big claims at the SOPA," Trixie said.

R - "I'm very serious right now. I'm not supposed to be telling you all this. Dante would be very mad at me. He's going to know," Rebeccah said.

T - "Okay, well, we need to go pay these bills before we get evicted Beccah and thanks a lot for helping us out. I promise to repay you somehow," Trixie said, tearing up.

R - "It's okay; you don't owe me anything. Let's put half of it up and head out. We are best friends and bandmates. Our success in life will depend on us working together. I'll ride or die for you, Trixie," Beccah said.

Scene 8 (Galaxy Zoo)

Mary had on blue sweatshirt and blue sweatpants. She was comfortable as she sat lotus-style. She was deep underground in the heart of the StarGaze Temple. In the center of the vast room was the golden, breathtaking, and marvelous throne. The throne was sitting atop a pyramid, elevated thirty feet.

Dio was dressed in all black, with his signature suit and sinister smile. He led her to the steps of the pyramid that led to the throne.

>D - "This is a long-awaited moment. I am proud to say welcome, Mary, and that's the last time I call you that. Once you sit on that throne, you will have a new title." Dio smiled.

>M - "I can't sit on the throne; it belongs to the Grand One. And I'm sure he'll be mad if I sit there," Mary said, looking up at the throne.

>D - "You are the Grand One. You actually found us before we had a chance to mount a search; your investigative journalist job takes you across the globe, I see," Dio said.

>M - "Wait… if I'm the Grand One, then why did you make me go through hoops at first? You could have just said that," Mary asked, the candles along the walls burned brighter as she raised her voice.

They both looked at the walls in disbelief at the strange interaction.

>D - "Okay, I'll admit that the knowledge I gave you is just the start to your better understanding as the Grand One of this generation. I apologize if it appears I misled you. But I just wanted to know you before your transition, you're a special woman," Dio said, forgivingly.

Mary looked at the throne in awe.

M - "So, what is so special about the throne, anyway? Is it
some kind of illusion or hologram?" Mary asked, skeptically.

She had the orb in one hand and the book in the other hand as she hesitantly
put her foot on the pyramid steps. The candles along the wall lit to their max-
imum flame as she stepped on the structure. She made her way up at a steady
pace, thinking her life is just a lie. Her eyes teared up angrily.

Mary approached the throne and looked back at Dio, who was kneeling,
watching her. She sat on the golden throne and the alien language that glowed
green on the book matched the orb. The contents of the book were becoming
clear as the alien language unraveled itself. It finally was in a human language
she could read. Mary laughed, which echoed.

D - "What is it, Grand One?" Dio asked.

M - "It's in Spanish. I just find that funny," Mary said.

D - "Can you speak Spanish?" Dio asked.

M - "Of course, now get off your knee, and please record this
moment with that camera there and do not mess up; I want
this recorded," Mary said.

Mary palmed the globe and sat the book on her lap and opened it to the first
page. The pages seemed to project from the book mid-air. The pages could
move like traditional paper, but it was a hologram projection that could be interacted with. Mary sat there with there, reading, and stopped after a while.

D - "What is it, Grand One?" Dio asked.

M - "It's an instruction manual on how to access the I.G.L.A
Starship Portal," Mary said.

She continued to read the projected page and then closed the book altogether.
She pressed on the orb that glowed simultaneously as her symbol did. The orb

was comprised of billions of small metal parts that quickly formed what appears to be a bracelet around her wrist, resembling an Apple Watch. She held her arm up to look at it in shock and awe.

She played with the advanced tech for around ten minutes and was amazed at its holographic screen it projected mid-air and she could manipulate it with her fingers, like a touch screen phone with no actual phone, just air. She knew this kind of technology didn't exist on earth at the moment, it was mind-blowing.

> M - "Okay, record this, I'm going to access the Portal. I don't know what's going to happen, so I order you to give this video file to Dante, so he knows, Beccah, too," Mary demanded.
>
> D - "Yes, Grand One, as you wish," Dio said, looking through the camera.
>
> M - "Okay, well, here goes nothing. Time to access the Portal to the I.G.L.A., and I don't even know what that means. But I feel like I should take that bold step if it's really destiny like you say it is," Mary said.
>
> D - "You are supposed to sit on humanity's highest throne," Dio said.

Mary nodded, then used the holographic keyboard to pull out the Portal which was nothing more than a simple bending of space and time. Her environment changed in the blink of an eye. She was aboard a spacecraft. The bright white, hospital like room had a wall that was completely transparent. It shown the planet Earth, which was big, as if it was in space nearby, which it was.

She then saw an astronaut walking towards her smiling, with her helmet removed from her suit. She had her hair braided and resembled the woman in her vision, her long-lost mother.

> MA - "Hello, my dear. Welcome to the I.G.L.A Grand station," Mother said, as white gas filled the room. "This gas is to rid your body of any viruses or bacteria that you brought

along with you from earth, unknowingly of course. We have a wide array of different life forms on the Grand station to protect."

M - "You look familiar. Where am I?" Mary asked, looking around.

Scene 9 (I.G.L.A. Grand station)

MA - "This is a planet-like Starship comprised of many sectors and environments. It can't be seen by the naked eye or satellite because it has a core comprised of dark matter, bending space time," Mother said. "Yes, to simply avoid unnecessary time wasting, I am your mother, and I never forgot about you, even though I've been far away," Mother said.

M - "I'm on a Starship called the I.G.L.A. Grand station, and it is like a planet with different kinds of life forms. Wow. When can I see a non-human? What does the I.G.L.A stand for? What's its purpose?" Mary asked. "What is the title of Grand One mean?" Mary excitedly asked, staring at the Earth from the transparent wall in the empty white room.

MA - "It stands for the Inter-Galactic Liaison Allegiance, and our job is to prevent life from being destroyed on many different planets and celestial bodies. And yes, you will meet an E.T in due time. It's very strange, and it may give you a heart attack," Mother said. "There are intelligent beings that take offense at being gawked at."

M - "I mean, I've watched a lot of aliens in movies, shouldn't I be more conditioned to actually seeing one?" Mary asked, her mother asked for her clothes only leaving her in her undergarments. She put on a white and orange space suit and the gas stopped pouring in.

MA - "You may be right my dear but first, the two of us are going to meet a few more humans and I'm going show you where we live on the I.G.L.A. Grand station. We have to go over a few things before you meet our fascinating neighbors, I have to brief you," Mother said.

They left the bright white room. The door was made of a liquid material that allowed them to walk through but turned metallic and opaque after they passed through it. The hallway interior was also white, as well, and didn't have any light fixtures as Mary expected it would. It was empty as they walked in the corridor of the Grand station to the I.G.L.A. Starship. They made their way to a black circular fixture on the wall, a Portal.

MA - "Get used to using Portals to travel, I'll slowly introduce you to the things you have access to, that Orb that transformed is a Portable Universal Super Computer, and it could do things that'll blow your mind. This isn't like the movies where it's all flashy; we like it simple in this area. Some life forms communicate using just radiation and some in frequencies only they can decipher," Mother warned.

M - "How many humans are on the Starship?" Mary asked.

MA - "Our sector is the Primate Sector, so there are different forms of Hominins and Hominids. But from our Earth, there are twenty-one of us: ten men and eleven women," Mother said. "As time goes by, you will learn more. This is a long journey."

Scene 10 (Time to Rock, Then Roll)

Dante was in the Fish Market District, in their safe house, he had Fatman with him. Dante had an assault rifle, loaded with nonlethal rounds and a .40 cal. with live rounds. They were counting money using two money counters and were stuffing money in a duffle bag.

> D - "Let's get out of here, Fatman; burn the rest of it," Dante said.

He burned down at least three, abandoned buildings in the Fish Market District and was putting the wraps on his final drug deal. He and Fatman jumped in a van and drove it to the old, abandoned bus station. Once they had the duffle bags of money secured in the trunk of the Beast, they poured gas on the van, leaving their old clothes in the gasoline-soaked van.

Fatman pulled out a lighter and was ready to light the fire when Dante gestured for him to stop. He then went to the trunk of the beast and lifted a grenade out and smiled. He cranked the Beast up and drove to a safe distance.

> FM - "Are you seriously gonna throw a frag grenade? This ain't *Call of Duty* fool. Where'd you get a grenade from anyway?" Fatman asked.

> D - "I got connections; just get inside of the Beast and watch this cool-ass explosion," Dante said, Fatman got into the car, shaking his head.

Dante hurled the grenade through the van's window and hopped inside of the armored sports car, watching the van violently and loudly explode into a big mushroom cloud of darkly colored smoke and bright orange fire. Glass and debris rained everywhere as Dante burned rubber and sped off. Fatman was just staring at Dante, who had a mischievous grin on his face.

> FM - "Damn! You're crazy as hell man, but that was cool. And if that truly was the last go, what happens now that we're

out of the game?" Fatman asked, listening to the police scanner, as well.

D - "Alright, from now on, our mission is to uncover the greatest mystery of all time, and we're gonna hide from the eyes of the law, hopefully. I have a plan, and I want you to be a part of it, my brother. I trust you with the lives of my sisters and mine, as well. You're my brother from another," Dante said, smoking a cigarette. "I need you on this one; we may have to beef with aliens." He laughed, swerving a little.

FM - "I'm down like the ground. You know I appreciate everything y'all done for me and my family. Your sisters are the most brave and smartest people I've run across, bro," Fatman said. "Beefing with aliens... please be joking, bruh."

D - "Dude, this is like a movie. We usually beef with the aliens, but we'll leave that to the author of this book. We need to visit Goldstein and give him this money to convert and pick up our last cash from the last job. Then we have to hit up the SOPA to watch the Pet Monkeys perform their set," Dante said.

FM - "The SOPA has their dance tonight? What we look like R. Kelly and Michael Jackson?" Fatman asked.

Dante laughed, wiping his eyes.

D - "So, which one of us is MJ cause they're both messed up," Dante asked.

Rebeccah, Trixie, and Rickey were at the SOPA's big gymnasium that the dance was being held in. They were setting up the equipment and did a sound check before any students came. Rebeccah was singing and playing the keyboard simultaneously, as she looked on the dance floor to spot Dante and Fatman two-stepping to her hard Rock and Roll. Her afro swayed as she sung.

The Pet Monkeys finished their song, and Beccah asked her audience of two if they wanted to Rock then Roll to her new song. Her duo audience clapped and screamed hell yeah. Beccah started the piano intro, and Trixie gave her a nice hip hop beat on her drums. Beccah was a good rapper and she let her lyrical skill show as she spit bars, tapping on the piano keys while holding the mic like a rapper.

After their rehearsal, a sweaty Beccah hopped off the stage and skipped to her brother, humming melodies. She gave the band the five-minute break hand signal as she bopped across the balloon strewn floor.

R - "So, how did you like that, we rocked that right?" Beccah asked, wiping her forehead. As a teacher strolled by.

D - "Yes, ma'am, killed it. I'm just glad I saw the raw performance," Dante said.

R - "So, you are gonna come watch the real deal show later?" Rebeccah asked. "I asked the principal if you could be my guests," Beccah said, tugging his arm.

D - "I don't have a date, Beccah, and as close to Fatman as I am, I didn't buy him a dress," Dante joked.

R - "It's cool because I took the liberty to ask Xi's daughter, Li-Chun, to be your date. I also told her to come dressed up and she accepted my invitation," Rebeccah said.

Dante looked a little nervous.

D - "Why would you do that? You know she has a big crush on me," Dante asked.

R - "So, who cares? You're a leader, a badass, and a rebel. Yet you're shy and intimidated by a pretty woman," Beccah teased.

D - "I'm not shy. I'm just not the romantic type. I know her very well, she's a hopeless romantic," Dante said.

FM - "Dude, it'll be good for you, tap into your sensitive side. I'm with Beccah on this one dawg. She looked out for you," Fatman said.

R - "Yeah, get over it, dude. She's waiting for you and you're going to be that gentleman we know you can be, hopefully," Rebeccah said, kicking a balloon.

FM - "I called my son's mother. She didn't go to our prom since she was preggo. So, I'm going to show her a good time tonight, we are partying Big Boss, we have to," Fatman said, happily. "It's in the script."

Dante shook his head.

D - "Okay, sh**, I'll go on this friendly date with Li-Chun, if it means that much to you two," Dante said, wanting to smoke at that point.

Scene 11 (Final Fantasy Prom 2176)

Dante was sitting on the hood of the Beast, smoking on a vape and waiting for Li-Chun to come from her nice condo in the Diamond District. It was seven that evening and the sun was starting to cascade over the neon-lit Diamond District streets that were not as full due to the cold weather.

He saw her come through the lobby and he hopped off the hood of his Mustang and put his vape up. She was a tall woman and very attractive, with flowing brown hair and brown eyes that were enchanting to look into. She had on a traditional Korean outfit, complete with a head piece. Dante sprayed a little cologne on before she approached. She smiled as she noticed his vape.

The tall, exotic woman gave Dante a hug, happy to accompany him. He hugged her back and loved the way she smelled. He indeed was a little intimidated by her, she had a presence that was stoic to him. She made him vulnerable because her vibes were enchanting and voice soothing. Making him let his emotional guard down. He helped her into the car as she reminded him of a Final Fantasy character. She reached over rubbing his arm as he drove to the SOPA.

LC - "I was so happy when your sister told me that you wanted to finally go out with me, and I really want to watch her perform for the school, too. I'm just happy that you invited me," Li-Chun said, her radiant eyes sparkled.

D - "Yeah, I'm glad you agreed to go. I thought a pretty lady like yourself would be spoken for," Dante said. "What about—?" Dante was cut off.

LC - "You have my full attention, when we are together there is no one else, I'm yours. I just want you to come around more often. What is it that I have to do to get your attention? I know you're here now, but it's been a while," Li-Chun said, rubbing his arm.

D - "It's not you at all. I told you that I'm a man that lives an edgy life, and I don't want you to get caught up in any of my activities," Dante said. "But let's not allow our past to get in the way of a great time. We are going to have a great time," Dante said.

As they sat at a red light, Li-Chun leaned over and gave him a peck on the cheek, making him smile and shake his head.

LC - "I see you aren't being shy now," the exotic woman said.

D - "I'm comfortable right now. You are just so beautiful and elegant, I don't want you to get hurt," Dante said.

LC - "I can handle myself, I'm a big girl. Just be you, I see you around all the time, you're really sweet. I can handle bullshit, sir," Li-Chun said. "I know more about you than you know."

They drove to the SOPA, and it took them an hour and a bridge trip to get there. They talked and had a deep conversation on the drive to the school. Dante wanted to have a calm, boring night with no surprises or revelations. But he knew that wasn't going to happen.

D - "Okay, well, if you know about me, hang on tightly," Dante said, speeding through the traffic.

LC - "See, we are going to be fine," Li-Chun said.

Scene 12 (The Pet Monkeys' SOPA Mosh Pit)

The dance had commenced, and Fatman and his longtime girlfriend, Pam, showed up with him dressed very conservatively, as well as Dante, who wore a nice sports coat. They got their wristband tickets and entered the gym and was met with loud, bass-filled music and strobe lights. Everything was going great; everybody was dancing and having a good time.

Dante and Li-Chun were getting punch and hanging out with Fatman and Pam. They let the kids have the dance floor as they played the sidelines. Keeping a good view of the stage, Li-Chun grabbed Dante's hand, so she could dance with him.

Rebeccah and her band were prepared, so they danced with their friends until it was time to take the stage. Mrs. Monroe gave them a lot of free will and control of the music that was playing. Rebeccah didn't dance crazily, she loved to just sway, moving to the beat. Trixie, on the other hand, had all of the moves. She was more energetic than her brother Rickey, who was dancing enthusiastically himself.

Mrs. Monroe and the Commissioner Captain Monroe, her husband, was there watching the party. Since they did have a daughter that attended the prestigious art school. Dante noticed that the captain was there as he danced with Li-Chun, who was showing Dante some of the new dance moves. He wondered if anyone else was going to pop out of the blue. He then saw the CEO of the *Freedom Journal*, the head editor, Lindsey Townsend.

He hugged Li-Chun so that so he could look for more people he would need to keep his eye on. Just as he looked, he heard the kids and staff clap and cheer as the Pet Monkeys took to the stage.

> R - "What's up, you guys? Y'all ready to Rock, or nah?" Beccah said, getting behind the piano to thunderous applause from her school.

She started to sing and play the keyboard at the same time, getting a lot of love from the big school. Their first song was heavy metal, with Trixie doing an awesome job of using bursts beats. They even had a PG-13 mosh pit; not really hardcore because they were just kids.

As they took an intermission between songs, Dante spotted Dio in his black tuxedo walking to him. Li-Chun saw his eyes and attention go to the mystery man in black. She knew that he was needed to talk to him, she knew of Dio from the articles Mary written on the StarGaze Society.

LC - "Go handle that and come back. Understand?" Li-Chun instructed him.

He kissed her cheek as Dante and Dio went out in the empty hallway to talk. Dante knew who he was and knew he needed to listen to him as it relates to his sister.

DIO - "I'm not going to hold up too much of our time, Mr. Dante. I've been instructed by your sister to give you something," Dio said.

He handed Dante an ordinary cellphone.

D - "Where is my sister, Dio?" Dante asked, getting straight to the point.

DIO - "If I told you, it would keep you from having a great time. So, just enjoy this nice dance and view the contents of this phone when you get home," Dio said. "I promise you; Mary is fine and in good care; she's safe."

D - "Alright, Dio, but don't play with me," Dante warned him.

DIO - "I wouldn't dare, Mr. Dante," Dio said. "We want the same thing.'

D - "What might that be?" Dante asked.

DIO - "Look at the phone later, then you'll get a better understanding of the situation," Dio said.

Scene 13 (The Primate Sector, The Mission)

Mary was in the Primate Sector of the I.G.L.A Starship. She was in her living quarters, which was a room with white walls and white floors and a bed that looked comfy, along with a shower and toilet in the middle of the room. There was a huge screen on the wall, but upon further inspection, it was a more of a projection on the wall. It was 3-D and could be manipulated.

Her mother shown her to her living quarters and Mary sat down on the bed, which had a very human Chicago Bulls blanket that belonged to her mother.

MA - "Okay, your room is designed for the human species of the primate spectrum. You have a shower in here, as well as a I.G.L.A super computer that you can use to access Portals and other parts of the Starship. "Your suit will clean itself, even if you don't take it off, as well as your boots; they automatically connect to your suit," Mother said.

M - "Okay. What about food? I'm kinda hungry, and can I not get weird alien food?" Mary asked, sitting on the bed. "I don't know how space travel works, but my stomach is rumbling," Mary said.

MA - "You have to access the terminal and order it; it is a protein-based food. Since this is the Primate Sector, most of us eat fruits and vegetables; try it out. It works on your Terminal watch, too, so you can easily access it. It'll arrive on the wall, via Portal," Mother stated, her voice was soothing. "I'm going to let you get accustomed to your room, then I'll let you meet some other humans in the sector," Mother said.

M - "Alright, but why am I here? How many different species exist on this artificial Planetary Starship? What's the mission?" Mary asked.

MA - "There are many species, as this is a big planetary structure. Once I take the parental lock off of your Terminal, you'll get a chance to find out," Mother said, kissing forehead. "You're here because you have a role to play, but please pace yourself, darling."

Her mother walked through the liquid metal door after waving her hand over a small green dot on the wall. The button allowed the door to become passable without even opening up, as it had no traditional knobs or hinges. She checked the room out and found some extra spacesuits hanging on racks and even some normal clothes and under garments. She took off her suit and got naked. As she took her watch off, it turned back into a blue orb that floated mid-air inside the glass shower structure beside her. The shower area was set up like a normal, modern Earth bathrooms in the small cube.

After she took a shower, she was mysteriously dry as she set foot on the floor. She found it warm as she put on the gray space panties and bra before putting her spacesuit on, which she found shockingly lightweight and comfortable, going barefoot in her personal room. She went to the Terminal projection on the wall and scrolled the menu to find somethings were blocked like Mother said.

Mary continued to scroll until she found the food option and pressed what she wanted in the air on the floating projection. She was starving and didn't know how much time passed since she left Earth, or if time was even a thing on the Starship.

Her food came through a small Portal on the wall by her small table with two chairs. Her table seemed to be made of wood and chairs, too; hints of earth. She ordered the fruit and veggie tray and loved how it looked: colorful, vibrant, and juicy.

After she ate, she got sleepy and climbed in the comfortable bed. She was both excited to start her journey, as well as feeling anxiety over the unknown. She was close to meeting aliens and primate beings from other planets and galaxies. Her role was unknown and small compared to the vast conspiracy she was undertaking.

Scene 14 (The Humans on the I.G.L.A.)

Mary awoken in her living quarters on the I.G.L.A Starship in her Spacesuit and boots, which apparently cleans itself. Mother came into the room via hologram on her Terminal. Only her face was shown in the clear HD hologram. She held her arm sideways to look at it.

MA - "How was your first day in the place that will become your home away from away?" Mother asked.

M - "I think the excitement level has risen. This is so unreal; my heart is beating really fast. Like, I'm not on Earth right now; that's strange," Mary said.

MA - "Good, put your boots on and activate the helmet from your terminal. Just scroll to the top, and it'll show your vitals, the status of the suit and the many options you have, including colors and symbols. You just have to be creative," Mother instructed via hologram.

Mary changed her suit color to pink and activated her helmet which was like an invisible barrier that formed around her head and the hologram of her mother ended. The helmet was strange, making her touch her head to feel her face. She saw words and info appear on the screen as she looked at things in the room, she even heard her mother's voice. Noticing her hologram in the corner of her eye.

MA - "Okay, now, go to the door and meet me down the C-1 corridor. I'll be waiting," Mother said.

Mary turned towards the door as the hologram left and the helmet call ended. She moved her hand over the green dot and the silver matte door turned to a blue looking liquid, letting her walk through it, and end up in the hallway that had huge window panels in place of the outer wall. She saw her mother on her Terminal, talking calmly to someone.

M - "Hello, Mother. Good morning, noon, night… What time is it?" Mary asked, groggily.

MA - "We have simulated twenty-four-hour days for the Primate Sector. Sleep every day and for a few hours is a common trait of apes. It would be morning for us, my dear," Mother said.

Mother used her Terminal and accessed the Portal section and picked one. The Portal was the standard black, void of sound and color, but big enough for them to walk through. They entered and was in the lab that belonged to the two Humans who overlooked it.

She saw an Indian man with long hair, reddish skin, and a traditional head garment. His partner was another North American Native; a woman with a dark complexion.

RL - "Hello, I'm Red Lightening, and I'm glad you're here. We've been waiting a long time for your arrival," Red Lightening said, a little star struck at the sight of the new human. "This is the Agriculture Department; we feed the Primate Sector and other sectors, as well," he said.

S - "Greetings, I'm Storm. Welcome aboard. It's a process, being new the first time on the Starship; you're never going to get used to it. But you're safe and mentally stable, so congrats. You are the Grand One, after all, like the books say," Storm said.

M - "I'm glad to be here; it's definitely a mental challenge. So, that food I ate came from you two in this lab?" Mary asked.

S - "Yes. We feed other sectors, too. The plant life grown here on the ship serves other purposes, Grand One," Storm said.

RL - "You'll learn how important it is to grow food as we get further in the script, this is all the author instructed me to say," Red Lightening said.

M - "I have to meet this author one day," Mary said.

Scene 15 (The Chase Part 1)

Dante had the phone that Dio gave him from earlier that evening. He finished the dance and even watched the Pet Monkeys perform. Everyone had a good time. Fatman and Pam left early to check on their son. Trixie, who behaved herself, was extremely good on the drums and Rickey had some killer riffs. They were tired afterwards as Beccah gifted them both $5,000 to help them out. Rickey drove Trixie and himself home. The dance was over. Rebeccah climbed into the backseat of the Beast, Dante helped Li-Chun in her seat, being a gentleman.

As they were going to get some pizza after the dance, Dante felt he was being watched and followed by a van. He sighed, as he realized that was the case. He saw Beccah following his gaze in the rearview mirror. Beccah pulled out a newer pistol this time, it was made for her small hands, but was still a powerful revolver.

D - "Li-Chun, stay calm. Beccah, don't look back or panic. I think we're being followed," Dante said. "I'm sorry—" Chun cut him off.

LC - "No need to apologize. It's not the worst thing that could've happen to us. We just have to get out of this safely," Li-Chun said, calmly, reaching under her seat, pulling a sub-machine gun out of her bag.

D - "What the f***? You brought a MAC-10 on our date?" Dante smiled, not knowing this side of Li-Chun.

R - "I like her; that's so cool. Can I hold it? You can hold my new .357 Mag," Rebeccah proposed.

D - "You two are crazy. I'm gonna lose them; they can't keep up with us. But just be ready, don't go shooting up the city, please," Dante said. "We don't want innocent people to get hit."

R - "Okay, but I will defend myself if I feel like I'm in danger," Beccah said, sitting low, keeping her head down.

Dante had an upgraded motor, so he did a quick turnaround in the middle of the lane and drove towards the van.

D - "Li-Chun, do exactly as I say. Give me your gun cocked back, off safety, and grab the wheel. Stay on the side of em'," Dante instructed.

He put the car in cruise control, heading towards the black van. He climbed through the window. His arm extended, holding the MAC-10. He shot the vans tires and engine, the black van swerved to avoid hitting the Beast. He made the van flip over and roll on its roof, sliding for a dramatically long-time and crashing into cars on the street. He climbed back into the Beast to see that Li-Chun was driving leaning over in her seat, smiling, biting her lip. Rebeccah was giggling, loving her brother's accuracy with the SMG.

D - "Okay, we are going to New Brington. I have an underground bunker beneath a house there. It's guarded and looked after by my own mercenary team," Dante said.

R - "When did you get an underground bunker, dude, with mercs and sh**? Bruh, that's so f***ing cool. I think I'm enjoying this too much," Rebeccah said.

D - "Beccah, calm down. Like I keep trying to tell y'all, I live a very dangerous life. But let's focus; we need to get there in one piece," Dante said.

LC - "I do have to admit that the part when the van flipped and slid on the roof for like sixty feet was kinda cool. I mean they were chasing us, no telling what they would've done if they caught up with us," Li-Chun said, rubbing Dante's arm. She was impressed by his actions when it mattered the most.

R - "I'm still hungry, though," Beccah said.

D - "We'll eat when we arrive in New Brington," Dante promised.

Scene 16 (The Chase Part 2)

Dante pulled up into the nice neighborhood and parked his '03 Mustang into the two-car garage. The garage had an armed merc guarding the door that led into the home. The merc had a long automatic rifle by his side. They made their way through the laundry room to get to the kitchen.

R - "I swear, if you tell me to open the fridge and it's a passage way underground, I'm gonna punch you," Beccah said.

D - "What? No, girl. We use the fridge to feed the people who are here throughout the day," Dante said. He pulled out some water and a box of Hot Pockets for them to heat up and eat.
They all sat quietly munching on the Hot Pockets and drinking water and after they were finished Li-Chun made a toast.

LC - "Toast to us making out of that alive, and I know you're a dangerous and mysterious man. So, toast to just a little info on what exactly is going on here. Dante, I need a briefing of some kind," Li-Chun said, seriously. Then she grabbed his shirt, pulling him towards her tall frame and kissing him, then pushed him back.

Rebeccah loved that emotional interaction as she had a big smile on her face.

D – "I'll tell you this… you're a super dope chick. I can't say too much about what we have going on right now. It's a must me and Beccah keep this secret, until we get a better grip on this. It's bigger than what you can even imagine," Dante warned.

D - "If I told you, it could endanger your life. And after our date, I think I want you around more. Now let's hit the Bat Cave."

He led them to a secret passage way behind the fire place in the living room and down into the underground bunker. They had cameras and lights that watched them as the descended the stairs to the bunker.

The underground facility had a huge room that was used as a lounging area, with a flat screen T.V. on the wall, with a round conference table and a map of the city. Blueprints to landmarks and government buildings were on the table. He had rooms in the bunker and a secret exit tunnel.

Dante took Beccah to his food storage room and closed the door behind them. Watching the video of Mary's last moment before she traveled through the portal. They were watching her sit on a golden throne with the huge temple walls glowing with candles. The gold throne sparkled atop of the pyramid structure.

They were open mouthed as Mary sat there opening up, what appeared to them to be, a Portal. Like they saw in sci-fi movies. She stood up and looked down at Dio. Then she gave the peace sign and slowly walked into the portal, and it quickly vanished.

R - "What in the f*** was that? Was that a portal?" Beccah whispered.

D - "I guess so. I assume she went off Earth or to another dimension. Let's keep this between us for now; this is crazy," Dante said.

Scene 17 (Fatman's Problem)

Fatman was with his son's mother, Pam, and their son, Frank, at their apartment in the busy Red-Light District. They lived in a regular building full of hipsters and college students, a very low-key place. Except when the frat brothers throw parties. Fatman hates the noise the students make, but Pam always tells him to let them have fun. She jokes that she knows all the new Hip-Hop music and dances; it makes the thirty-four-year-old feel young.

They were all in the living room watching T.V., and Fatman was eating a bag of chips as Pam walked in. He patted the seat by him, wanting her to sit down, and she did, sighing.

> FM - "You don't have to do all that. I know we might not be on the best terms, but I still love you. That's why I invited you to the SOPA dance. If you said no, I would not have gone," Fatman said.

> P - "Don't try anything. Just because you behaved yourself and did a nice thing, you still cheated and took me for granted. And that's why you sleep out here on the couch," Pam said, rubbing Frank's curly hair.

> FM - "I really do appreciate you; I just don't show it properly. But I do love you," Fatman said, he quickly pushed her to the floor along with Frank and shielded them with his large frame as gunshots tore up the apartment. "Remember what I've taught you what to do in moments like this... don't panic."

Fatman and his family crawled as quickly as they could to the bedroom, where Fatman kept his guns. He followed behind and looked to him for guidance as this was not his first shootout. He found his silver Beretta in the dresser drawer and was determined to get his family out of this dangerous situation alive.

> FM - "Okay, they know we are here, so I'm probably sure there's gonna be at least five or six guys. If they want us dead,

I'm gonna start crawling towards the door stay low and crawl behind me. I will get us to safety," Fatman said.

He crawled along the floor as the automatic shots rippled through their apartment, sending dust, glass, and pillow feathers in the air. He made it to the bedroom door and didn't hear gunshots. But he did hear the stomping of boots.

FM - "Go hide in the tub, lay down, and be quiet," Fatman instructed them. They did and he went and flipped over the dinner table and crouched behind the table waiting on the team of hitmen to breach his apartment. He had plenty of training with Dante, so he was confident.

The front door flew open with a flash bang that temporarily affected his hearing, but not vision. He shot the first intruder in the head. Chunks of brain and blood splattered the eyes of the next man in the assault and briefly blinded him. Fatman shot him in the visor of his tactical helmet. The next two men who came in were treated to a barrage of pistol rounds as Fatman quickly leaped over the table. Grabbing one of the dead hit man and used him as a human shield, killing two more intruders in the hallway as they shot anyway despite their fallen comrade's body.

Fatman called Dante and told him what just happened and that he was headed to the bunker through the emergency back entrance. He got his family, and they left the building, stepping over the dead bodies and covering Frank's eyes, so he wouldn't see the bloodshed. Fatman got everyone outside, and they took cover behind a car. There was one more assassin in the form of a sniper. He picked up a piece of glass that fell from his apartment and tried to locate the sniper's location.

He spotted the muzzle flash as the sniper tried to fire on them through the car. He wanted a good shot and needed a diversion. He moved to another car drawing the fire away from his family. He looked at Pam, who looked afraid.

Fatman motioned for her to be still, he counted the time between shots to determine it was a bolt action rifle. He stood up to get the guy to shoot, before quickly kneeling back down. After counting in his head, he stood back up emptying his Beretta in the hitman's direction and watched the guy fall over the balcony. He guided his family to his GMC SUV, and they got in. He ran to check the body, to get any clues of who his assassins were and looked under the SUV for explosives. He took a dog tag and a cellphone, finding no explosives.

He then drove to the New Brington suburb bunker and entered through the secret back entrance for vehicles, looking like the bat cave because of its dark gray concrete walls. He sat in the SUV with his family for a minute.

FM - "Pam, baby, I'm so sorry. Frank, I'm sorry, son. I promise we are going to find out who was responsible for that, and they will pay," Fatman said calmly. Dante ran to the passenger side, checking on Pam and Frank. He hated that they went through that.

P - "We'll talk about that later. Right now, I need a shower and a smoke. Having a team of hitmen shoot up your home is very nerve-wracking, and where the f*** are we? It looks Batman is going to pop up any minute," Pam said as Dante opened her car door.

D - "I heard what happened. I promise you, it's okay. You can relax here. Me and Fatman got it covered here. Frank, are you alright, man?" Dante asked.

F - "Yes, Uncle Dante, it was like a video game, and Daddy had his big pistol, shooting them like pow, pow, pow," Frank said, demonstrating his father's actions.

P- "Frankie, baby, that wasn't a video game. We could've died or gotten really hurt, but your daddy saved us. He was heroic, and I'll never forget that," Pam said.

Li-Chun and Rebeccah came to get Pam and the small boy, to take them up to the house, to shower and eat. Pam noticed the look on the women's faces. They went through something similar, looking fatigued.

P – "So, they tried to kill all of us tonight, huh?" Pam asked Li-Chun, as they moved through the bunker. Leaving Dante and Fatman, to talk amongst themselves.

D - "Man, I'm glad you're okay, dude," Dante said, dapping him up and hugging his brother from another. "I promise to put a bullet in the head of whoever is responsible for this. How many guys you killed in all?" Dante asked, he wasn't one to stray away from violence.

FM - "I counted seven bodies. Did you rack up a body count?" Fatman asked.

D - "Nope. We went on a high-speed chase, with a little shootout on some Vin Diesel ****. I tried to avoid casualties. I just want to know who sent them after us?" Dante asked, as Fatman handed him the dog tags and cell phone.

FM - "We have a very nice computer here. Let's run a background check on him and see what's on the phone," Fatman said.

D - "Good, and I when find out who did this, I promise payback. Now, let's get to work, then. I want to knock on some doors." Dante smiled.

FM - "Okay, let's get to it. Because they tried to kill me and my family, I promise this won't sit well with me. I want to put a bullet in the top guy," Fatman said angrily.

Mary was aboard the I.G.L.A. Planetary Starship in the Agriculture Sector. She was with her mother and the two Humans, Red Lightening and Storm, Egyptian farmers. They went through another Portal to end up in a vast field of many different types of veggies and trees with fruit. The field had a ceiling made of a shiny metal, making her feel warm, inspecting the veggies.

RL - "We feed the Primate Sector and use the oxygen the plants create," Red Lightening said.

S - "We also utilize the many oils the plants make. Organisms on the Starship use our products," Storm said.

M - "Are these plants from Earth? Are there alien fruit in the big field?" Mary asked, in awe.

S - "Yes, these plants and some trees are from Earth, but there are countless, Earth-like planets in this universe that bear fruit, and when you say alien, other species look at us Humans as alien, if it helps," Storm said. She held up her palm and a small Portal appeared and quickly disappeared dropping a black pear off in the air, which landed in her open palm. She gave it to Mary.

M - "What is it? Can I eat it?" Mary asked. Storm nodded and she took a bite. The center was white and full of juice.

S - "It's a fruit that grows on a moon around Jupiter; it has a nice story behind it. But that's a story for another time. You have to meet other people as you get accustomed to the Planetary Ship," Storm said.

Mother then opened up another Portal that took them to another facility. It was a room that had blue floors that moved like water; the walls and ceiling were black and void of color. A table sat on the medium-sized square floor. Mary looked around and there were no walls at all; the light blue floor appeared to have borders that connected to nothing visible. Two Indian people in their signature Human Spacesuits came up to greet them and explain the blue floor suspended in space.

T- "Hello, I'm Taj, and this is my wife, Pryai. We oversee the Research and Development Sector. You are witnessing new technology we developed for the terminal watches, such as the one you're wearing. You'll be able to access it soon," Taj said.

M - "So, what exactly does this area represent? Are we in space with some kind of force field around it? Let me guess… the technology you've developed is using Portal technology in some kinda way," Mary inquired.

P - "Yes, we are literally in space in a medium-sized room, but what you call a force field is actually that. I see your Earth is familiar with it," Pryai said.

M - "Wow, that's so cool, what else can my Terminal do?" Mary asked.

T - "It has a purpose that is quite amazing, I'm going to let the training teach you all of its functions, so you can use it properly," Taj said.

Scene 19 (The Primate Associates)

Mother opened another Portal; this one was blue. They walked through it and ended up in a black void. Mother put her hand on Mary's shoulder and looked at her in an intense way.

M - "What is it, Mother? Is everything alright?" Mary asked. She knew the black void was important.

MA - "Yes, I'm fine. After seeing you interact with the Ship and your curious nature, I'm going to let you meet more of the Primates. I'm going to introduce you to a close friend of mine. To be blunt, this will be your first encounter with intelligent life different from what you've known. He knows you're going to stare at him. He is magnificent to look at, from an earthling myself, but the reveal itself has killed a few humans giving them heart attacks and even causing them to commit suicide," Mother said, rubbing her shoulder.

Mary took a deep breath and let it out, her suit got a little cooler as she got hot and sweaty. She could feel her face cooling off at the same time. She nodded, and Mother closed the Privacy Portal and they were in a savannah-like grassland, with a huge tree, that bore fruit. The tree had a majestic look to it and Mary was feeling at home, strangely

She then saw a huge gorilla run on all four limbs to them, she got extremely nervous, and her heart beat rose, showing in her Helmet vitals. She stood her ground as the huge gorilla got closer, she noticed it was a male and he was smiling. He got within twenty feet and stood up on his legs, towering over her and Mother.

T - "So, this is the Grand One. Hello, fellow Earthling, I'm the Grand One from another Earth in the Multiverse. My name is Titan," Titan stated, in his deep voice, he softly hugged Mother.

Mary was completely in awe of the huge gorilla, who had sat down to appear less frightening to the new comer. Mary stared at the gorilla, and she instantly felt as if everything she learned on her planet was a lie and that the Humans were sheep, lost to the grand mystery of the universe and what's in it. She managed to not faint or pass out. Just staring at the talking gorilla, with huge muscles and intelligence.

M - "You're from Earth, too; from an alternate universe. Do Humans live on your planet?" Mary asked.

T - "Yes, Grand One. Humans live on my planet, but our social structure is the opposite of your planet. The primates and monkeys are the intelligent ones, and the Humans are in the zoos. Let's go to my reflection area, and I'll explain in more detail," Titan proposed.

M - "Wait, I want a hug, too. I love gorillas, and I've never been this close to one in my life," Mary said.

Titan let the small Human woman hug him, and she didn't feel threatened by the gorilla who, technically speaking, was an alien because his existence further proves her Earth isn't the only host of intelligent life.

MA - "You seem to be taking this well. I'm glad to see that. I have a lot of faith in you, my child," Mother said.

Scene 20 (The Missing Link)

Titan, Mary, and Mother sat around a fire in the habitat Titan lived in.

M - "Okay, I know that the many galaxies and Multiverses contain various forms of life, but I have a big one for you to explain to me," Mary requested, sitting on a tree stump. "Human beings on my planet."

T - "The origin and beginning of mankind… well, since Mother knows more than I, she should be the one to speak, Mother," Titan said, tinkering with his terminal, which he wore around his head.

MA - "Okay, well, the answer is very simple. Evolution occurs naturally on the Earth as it always has, with exceptions. Primate evolution on our Earth was manipulated two million years ago, when a super advanced group of beings from a long dead planet, restructured the DNA of the ape-like creatures and created the first humans, giving a little knowledge as an experiment," Mother said.

M - "I've seen that in movies, certain people back home believe that. All they need is confirmation on their Ancient Astronaut Theory," Mary said.

MA - "Humans won't take that revelation well," Mother said, the fire casting shadows on their suits. "That timeline played out in the Multiverse on a parallel Earth and they eventually nuked the planet, slowly destroying it. We have to keep the secret from them, we've intercepted mankind's radio signals that they've sent out in Space, just to prevent them from finding intelligent life. Earth tech can't bypass our most basic barriers," Mother said.

M - "I can ask all the questions about Humans, but I want to know what's the big picture. What is the I.G.L.A. as it relates to me? What about the Star Killers?" Mary asked.

MA - "Good question. I'll say that the same aliens that are capable of advanced cosmic physics and can manipulate DNA, also try to destroy Solar Systems," Mother stated. "They are dangerous aliens who don't value life and will seek to destroy entire Galaxies and we can't allow that. We know that these rogue Star Killers are already practicing this destruction. We assembled this Planetary Ship to hold all the life from as many planets and moons just in case they are destroyed. We must hunt and monitor the Star Killers," Mother explained.

M - "Wow, that's a lot. That's crazy. So, what is my role in all of this? I mean, I'm not even a scientist or astrobiologist; I'm just a journalist," Mary said.

MA - "You're more than just a journalist and my daughter. Your detective skills and investigative background will come in handy. Instead of war zones on Earth, you'll be in war zones in the vast cosmos to save the life that sometimes leads to the creation of more life. I support this grand mission with my life and I'm asking you to follow in my footsteps?" Mother asked.

Scene 21 (Grand Cellphone Coverage)

Dante and Fatman were inside of the bunker, sitting inside of an armored GMC truck. Dante had doubts about leaving the women behind, so he got out of the SUV.

FM - "What's the problem, bruh? The girls and Frank will be fine, let's go unravel the clues to find these a**h*les and end them," Fatman said.

D - "I don't think that's a good idea. We don't need to put more of our family and friends in danger. I'm just going to facetime Goldstein and see what the crazy Jew has to say. We're safe here; nobody knows about the bunker," Dante said.

The cellphone Dio gave him started to ring, he looked at it and quickly answered it.

D - "Hello. Dio, is this you?" Dante asked.

D - "Yes. I need to be brief. I know you were attacked earlier, and you want answers," Dio said, reassuringly and briefly. "The people that sent those assassins are a terror Cult called the Mercury Order, they also possess alien artifacts. After your sister assumed her role as the Grand One, the technology they have has been activated. In conjunction with other alien tech, they need the part you have. They will hunt you down for it," Dio said.

D - "Mary's role is what?" Dante asked.

D- "Your sister is the Earth's Grand One, one of the few chosen Humans. She is to protect this planet and others like it. Meet me at the StarGaze Temple at exactly 12:30 P.M., and I'll answer your questions in person. Somethings are hard to explain on the phone. For now, hold your position and be patient," Dio said, ending the call.

Dante hung the phone up and looked at Fatman, who was standing with folded arms and a quizzical look on his face.

FM - "What is it?" Fatman asked. "I need the truth, my brother."

D - "Well, we are being pursued by the Mercury Order and they won't stop no matter the cost. We have something they want, and they also have alien artifacts. They manipulate the artifacts, yet they don't work properly unless they have all the remaining artifacts to combine together. I know where one of the artifacts are; we need to get the other pieces, all of them," Dante said.

FM - "Okay, you were just talking to a member of the Star-Gaze Society. Do we work for them because they are powerful people?" Fatman asked.

D - "We have to work with them. Dio is his name, and he knows exactly what we need to do so we can contact Mary. So, in a way, we are officially working alongside the StarGaze Society," Dante said.

FM - "Wait, we are working for a cult?" Fatman asked.

D - "Yes, and I have to warn you, it's going to get crazy. You'll be under a lot of mental stress and fatigue, so buckle up," Dante warned.

Scene 22 (Crossroads)

The four of them sat in the high-tech living room, underground in the bunker. They were comforting each other.

D - "Alright, y'all," Dante said, getting their attention. "I have strong evidence that our assassination attempts were by the Mercury Order. They are very good at killing their targets," Dante said. "They have very good weapons and funding," Dante said.

Li-Chun changed from her dress into some blue jeans and a black leather jacket over a white shirt.

LC - "So, what do they want from us? I mean, I would hate to die or shoot someone over something I don't know that much about," Li-Chun said, arms folded.

D - "I promise, no one will hurt you. We will protect you until this Mercury Order thing is over," Dante said. "It's a secret that we will have to fight to keep secret. It may sound crazy, but you not knowing a lot is protecting you. Do you trust me?" Dante asked, moving towards her, and holding her hands, unfolding her skeptical arms.

She looked at him with a serious look on her face, exhaling deeply. He hugged her and kissed her cheek.

D - "So, tonight, we stay here and gather our thoughts, and remember, nobody can know where we are, lie to them if you have to. There are beds everywhere in the house; rest up. You'll be safe," Dante said to everybody.

Later that night, Dante sat in front of a laptop, smoking a blunt. Everyone was all throughout the house, relaxing in their rooms. Pam even let Fatman sleep in the bed next to her and Frank. Pam gained all new respect and trust for him as he protected them and was amazing to watch in the stressful, scary time. Beccah was on the phone talking to Trixie; she had on blue Elmo pajamas. Sitting lotus style, laughing, and joking.

Li-Chun walked downstairs to the bunker and found Dante smoking and listening to some music. Li-Chun strolled over to him and sat on his lap. She hugged his neck, leaning over to kiss him. He stopped her with his finger on her lips.

D - "Are you sure you want to do that?" Dante asked. "You know what you're getting into?"

LC - "I should be asking you… are you ready?" Li-Chun said, removing his finger from her face and leaning forward, her forehead touching his. "Stop being so hard to get and just relax. All that action from the chase and shootout has me feeling some type of way," Li-Chun said.

Dante wrapped his arms around her waist, pulling her closer to him, kissing her. He felt someone watching them, so he looked around to see Beccah hiding behind a corner.

R - "I'm sorry, I forgot my charger," Beccah said. She really didn't mean to interrupt.

D - "Well, don't sneak around like that," Dante said, as Li-Chun sat on the desk, embarrassed at being caught by his young sister.

ACT 2

Scene 23 (The Strange Jellies)

Mary and Mother were in a Privacy portal. Mother was showing her how to access her waterproof suit function. Mary looked at her suit, which seemed to get tighter. Her Helmet was invisible to her and weightless also. It was displaying real time information at whatever she looked at. She looked at her mother and could see her vitals and suit information. Mother looked at her, waiting for Mary to say she was ready. Mary nodded, and Mother waved her right hand and opened another Portal.

Mary had a fear of the ocean and being underwater. She was very hesitant, but her mother gave her a reassuring look and that made her walk towards her as they both walked into the Portal. They emerged in a bright blue ocean and there was a lot of underwater vegetation, but no fish in sight. Mother went over to a floating Mary and grabbed her hand; she was surprised she could hear her mother talking to her.

> MA - "You're fine. You can move the same way out of water as you can in water, but faster. Just relax," Mother instructed. "You are going to enjoy the journey."

Mary moved through the water effortlessly, she smiled at how much fun she was having with her mother. She didn't move in a swimming motion, but almost as if she was flying. She noticed the coral reef had bright colors, along with strangely shaped organisms that dominated the sea floor. She read the analysis on her live data streaming Helmet interface and was stunned at the different biosignatures. Her mother was leading her through the bottom of the ocean on the Planetary Ship.

> M - "These coral reefs are from the Planet Syrux and have a lot of cool abilities. They are apparently key to the survival of the very large jellyfish-like creature called the Zylux and they—" Mary was cut off by a huge, transparent jellyfish that had sparks of electricity coursing through its body and tentacles.

The jellyfish-like creature raised one tentacle, and electricity shot off from the end of its raised tentacle. A penny-sized ball of sparks slowly floated just in front of Mary; her jaw dropped, stunned at the giant creature. The penny sized ball of spark then formed being displayed in her helmet saying: "Hello, Human, welcome to the remaining portion of my lost sea Planet Syrux. I'm Zylux.

Mary got over her shock of the intelligent, colossal jellyfish since they looked similar to the ones on her Earth. Her helmet interface shown the intel and story of the destruction of Syrux. Mary could communicate by sending an Electric Message because the being receive them through the sea.

M - "I'm Mary, I'm from Earth. Well, one of many Earths, apparently. I'm the new fish," Mary joked, making the large jellyfish send another small shock bubble.

Z - "Nice one. LOL. You are just like your mother," Zylux said.

M - "So, can I have the story of how you arrived on the Planetary Ship?" Mary asked, surprised it knew human slang.

MA - "Of course. Since your first mission will be on a need-to-know basis involving the Syrux destruction," Mother said, stepping in.

Dante and Li-Chun were in the Red-Light District, leaving the others in the heavily fortified underground bunker in New Brington. The two of them were zigzagging through traffic on a very fast motorcycle. Li-Chun was on the back, with her helmet on over her long black, silky hair flowing in the wind, holding onto Dante very tightly.

Dante got a possible sighting of a Mercury Order member and he trailed them and to get whatever info he could on them. Li-Chun wanted to piece together the situation also, finding an excuse to hang out with Dante, doing crazy and criminal things. Li-Chun is very a stoic and calm person under stressful situations, so she meshes well with Dante, who was just as unbothered and nonchalant as her.

They sped through a side alley, driving into a parking lot garage, speeding to the top. They got off of the motorcycle and went over to the ledge and sat behind strategically placed cars. He pulled out a small bag from the back of the car, removing binoculars, looking over the ledge, down towards the ground below them.

LC - "Are we going to kill the guys who tried to kill us?" Li-Chun asked as she screwed a suppressor on the tip of her small Uzi, which also a flashlight on the bottom.

D - "No, Li-Chun baby. Do you normally take compact pistols and tactical equipment with you on dates? Because this is just a recon mission, not the attack. We don't know enough about them. They are strong and outnumber us. We have to kill the head person in charge," Dante said, scanning the area. He focused on a subject on the streets below.

D - "It's the Commissioner, Captain Monroe, with the Mercury Order, in their navy-blue suits and red ties," Dante said. "They are getting in the cars. Let's get in a car and trail them." Dante put up his binoculars. "We follow and watch that's it. I'm not in the mood for another shootout in broad daylight."

They went to a Dodge Hellcat and got in. They went down the many garage levels and onto the street. A few cars behind the three-car enemy caravan. They followed them throughout the crazy, dense traffic, until they arrived at the Downtown Jewelry District, parking on the opposite side of the road.

Dante pulled a pistol from the glovebox and put a suppressor on it. He pulled out a long clip and handed it to her. She looked at the magazine and bullets in a funny way.

> LC - "Damn, Dante, baby non-lethal rounds. What the f***, man? These people tried to kill us just the other day," Li-Chun said, quizzically.

> D - "Just relax. We can't kill anyone with the Commissioner here, and I also need information. They are more useful to us alive, for the moment. I do like that you are ready to lay these a****les down. That's hot," Dante said.

He watched them go into a coffee shop: the Commissioner and the Mercury Order leader, who wore a blue suit and red tie, their signature look. They had six security guards with them. Dante kept a low profile.

Scene 25 (Mercury Stuntman Assassin) Part 2

Dante needed to get an ear in that cafe quick, and Li-Chun offering the first ideas coming across her mind didn't help at all. He kissed her to make her gasp. She blushed and stopped talking, allowing him to focus. He called his tech-guy, Gun, the Korean car technician,

> D - "Hey, what's up, bro? I got a few questions if you're not busy," Dante asked, nodding his head. "Alright, I have to listen to the Commissioner and a Mercury Order Captain. I have my hacker iPhone and my laptop with me, and it's cut on," Dante said.

Dante had the laptop on Li-Chun's lap, letting her control it. She was listening to his conversation on speaker phone. She took notes on her phone, as well, so she could she could use this technique herself later.

> D - "The problem is that I can't go in the cafe, and I can't send my partner in. They wouldn't keep talking, but it is an Internet café," Dante stated.

> G - "Open the photo app on the laptop I gave you. It should bring up the tool that you can use to secretly take over somebody's laptop or device. You can use the same app to measure the distance from you and the cafe to narrow the search," Gun said on the speaker phone.

Dante watched Li-Chun type on the laptop very fast, with her black hat on, trying to be low-key. She smiled at how easy it was, judging how far the cafe was from their location. It was around sixty feet, in her judgement.

> LC - "Okay. I got one really close to him. It says I have two good options: a camera or voice. It's up to you, sir," Li-Chun presented the options.

D - "Let's go with audio. Gun, thanks, bruh. I'm going to send something your way when I get back," Dante said.

G - "I know. That's why you're the man. Be safe and hit me up whenever you need me. Peace," Gun said, ending the call.

Dante then listened to the convo between Captain Monroe and the Mercury Order Cappo.

D - "Record this," Dante instructed Li-Chun.

—— Hacked Convo—-

CM - "Listen. I saw how you handled our situation the other night; you disappointed me. I believed in you," Capt. Morgan said, sipping his coffee.

XO - "That was a mistake. I understand your frustration. But remember who you are talking to. Your badge can't protect you from us if we wanted to bypass you. But I do respect you a lot, so I'll forgive you this time," X.O. said.

CM - "You get one more chance to take care of all of them. Or we cut your funding," Capt. Monroe said. "I want them all gone; the kid, too."

Dante and Li-Chun looked at each other and he sent out a code red back to the bunker to Fatman, so he could put the mercs on alert mode and to watch over their families.

Dante and Li-Chun drove to Mary's apartment on the motorcycle, parking in the alley by the restaurant's side entrance. Dante saw one of the Mercury Order members across the street. Li-Chun got very mad. She knew that they wanted to hurt the people in the building to get at them.

She saw what she thought for sure was some kind of explosive being put in a backpack by one of the Mercury Order goons. She pulled out her machine pistol with the silencer and non-lethal rounds. She shot at the man in the navy suit and red tie and his partner, too. They both dropped to the ground. She ran over and grabbed the backpack and looked inside.

Dante heard footsteps; he turned around, punching a Mercury agent, sneaking up on them, knocking the attacker out. He took his cellphone and gun from his unconscious body and dragged him to the alley, putting him in the dumpster. The scared citizens all fled the scene in front of the Pearl Garden.

He ran with Li-Chun inside of the restaurant and made sure all of the employees left and went home. She had no choice but to do so. Li-Chun put her pistol back in her purse and was a little calmer, ashamed for having to shoot those agents in front of her father, Xi.

> LC - "Dad, get Oma and little brother and leave for our home in New Brington, it's not safe here. It's going to be a crime scene. Please go and take this with you," Li-Chun said, giving him a small pistol. Hugging and kissing her father.

> D - "No. They'll be much safer if you take them and protect them. He'll need your skills, trust me," Dante said, he leaned over kissing her on the cheek.

She nodded and helped them out the back door. Dante went back outside and hopped on his motorcycle and took off down the street. He zig-zagged through traffic, spotting four motorcycles chasing him. He smiled at his typical car chase through broad daylight. He drove on the opposite side of the road, dodging traffic as he flew like a shot rocket. One of the goons tried to do the same driving technique as Dante, but ended up hitting a truck, flying through the air.

He still had to shake the remaining three motorcycles, who were right behind him. Dante drove through alleys, approaching a garbage truck. He popped a wheelie and aimed for a trashcan in the street. The back wheel touched the ground and hit the garbage can, sending the motorcycle flying over the garbage truck like Motocross. He then heard the three bikes crash into the truck as he landed his bike on the back of a flatbed truck.

He burned out, launching off the back of the flatbed and onto the hood of a car. That same car aggressively knocked him off of the bike, sending him sliding across the street. The car pulled up beside him and the captain got out with a pistol in his hand, ready to shoot him.

CM - "I'm sorry, Dante, but you know too much. I'm going to have to kill all of you to keep this secret," Capt. Monroe said, pointing the gun at him.

Just as Captain Monroe was about to pull the trigger, his arm was shot, and he dropped the gun. Dante then got up and knocked out the captain, taking his phone, wallet, and badge. He injected the captain with a syringe to keep him unconscious for a while.

He saw that the person who saved his life was Li-Chun. He limped over to her, and she helped him into the car. They drove to New Brington and went to Li-Chun's parents' big suburban home. Dante had two black SUVs out in front of their driveway. Two teams of mercs were in the trucks and they were low-key but armed to the teeth.

Li-Chun, who was a tall and strong woman, helped Dante into the house. As a mercenary stood guard on the porch, Xi took a look at Dante's ribcage in the kitchen and Li-Chun helped her father by boiling herbs and wrapping Dante's midsection up.

X - "I don't want to know what's going on. But I want it re-solved and I want my name clear," Xi said. "You have some bruised ribs; they may be broken or fractured. You're going have to relax, young man," Xi instructed.

D - "Thank you, Xi. Li-Chun, can you help me to the couch? I need to rest up," Dante said, as Xi left.

LC - "Better idea; I have plenty of room in my bedroom. Plus, I'm going to have to look after you. So, come on, I promise I won't bite. Unless you like that kind of thing," Li-Chun said, blushing.

Rebeccah pulled out boxing gloves, and Fatman shook his head. She put the gloves on, and Pam put hers on, as well.

P - "Watch Mama, son, you could learn something. I used to box back in the day, that's how I met your daddy," Pam said, showing her foot work.

FM - "Okay, ladies, don't bruise each other up; just simple sparring. Remember Pam, Beccah is just a kid," Fatman said.

B - "She may have height and reach over me, but I'm quick on my feet," Beccah said.

They began the sparring session in the underground bunker, and it started off with both of the women showing their speed off. Beccah had a slight advantage in speed, due to her youth. Beccah took some of the body shots because she wanted to stay close to Pam.

It appeared as if Pam was overwhelming Beccah. Fatman was close to stopping them. Yet he continued to watch as Beccah held her arms together, protecting her body; she smiled. Pam eventually got tired, and Beccah seized the opportunity by striking as Pam tried to move back. That made Pam vulnerable. Beccah landed some big punches in combination and rhythm, exactly where she wanted on Pam's torso. Pam fell on her ass, and Fatman didn't intervene. Pam got up and got back in her stance, realizing that a seventeen-year-old girl just rope-a-doped her.

P - "Good stuff, girl. Show me what else you got, Rebeccah," Pam said.

Pam couldn't let the young girl whoop her. But it is was a little hard because Beccah was short and stout. Rebeccah was strong and had muscles from her guitar and tennis playing.

Rebeccah just focused on blocking and avoiding the quick jabs from the stronger older woman, who could box. Beccah just had to be careful in the second half of the fight. Pam was going on the offensive. After dodging Pam for two minutes, Beccah hit her once on her bruised elbow once and Pam stopped the sparring.

P - "You are too calculated. This was just supposed to be a sparring match; you targeted a bruise. That's not fair," Pam complained.

B - "I apologize. You are so much stronger than me, I couldn't let you keep hitting me. I had to take advantage of your weakness," Beccah said as she hugged the taller woman. "My brother taught me to always find the weak spots in your opponent. Just like that time those two guys caught me in the alley and tried to assault me," Rebeccah said, taking off the gloves.

P - "I'm not familiar with that story. What happened to them? You don't have to tell the story, if you don't want to," Pam asked, sitting down on the bunker's living room couch.

R - "It's crazy, but they had me pinned down, and I had got one of my hands free and grabbed my knife from my bra and did what my brother taught me... I stuck the knife deep in the man's neck and warm blood squirted on my face, and that's when the other man took off running, so I threw my knife into his back, and he pleaded for his life," Beccah said.

P - "You didn't kill him, did you?" Pam asked, covering her mouth. Listening to the innocent looking girl with the big afro tell the sad and violent tale.

B - "No. I should have though. I just broke his arm and made him apply pressure on the other man's neck until the ambulance came. Dante was mad at me. He wanted me to leave them to die in that alley; I was young. But now, I would've just shot them once in the head and put their bodies in the sewer," Beccah said.

P - "Oh, my God. Rebeccah, why would you say that?" Pam asked.

R - "Because a month later, my brother was in an abandoned building in the Fish Market District. Doing whatever s*** he does, and they caught them in the act of trying to sexually assault another teen girl. Dante did some horrible things to them that I can't say. I can't forgive myself for that happening to that girl," Beccah said.

Later on that night, Beccah called Trixie and talked to her for a few minutes and learned of a motorcycle chase with a few casualties that happened in the city earlier. Beccah smiled, thinking of her brother, doing movie stunts on a motorcycle through traffic and flying over s***, as he did exactly just that. She hung up the phone, wanting to see her friend so badly.

Scene 28 (Mercury Stuntman Assassin) Part 5

Dante was laying in Li-Chun's bed that night after an action-packed day. He laid there thinking about his next move. Li-Chun was taking a hot shower, and fifteen minutes later, she was strutting in black silk pajamas and stretching out on her couch, in the corner of her room.

D - "You don't have to sleep on the couch; you could lay next to me," Dante said.

LC - "I would love to. But you're hurt; you don't need any excitement. We need our leader healed up and ready to tell us our next moves. I will lay with you when you heal up," Li-Chun said, pulling a blanket over herself. "Now, goodnight. Get some sleep. I know you're going through a lot and I'm not trying to strain our strange relationship. But I do love you," Li-Chun said, flipping T.V. channels to watch the news.

D - "I love you, too. I've always tried to avoid getting you in-volved in my lifestyle because it would get dangerous. Even back in the day during our prom, I was in the middle of a shootout and got hit in the leg," Dante said. "I broke up with you to keep you safe, Xi talked to me, as well, and I thought it would be better if we kept our distance. Now, you're back in my life and you carry guns now. You shot the police captain in the arm with accuracy; that's girlfriend material;" Dante joked.

LC - "Wait, are you saying that you want me to be your girl-friend? Because I'm totally down. I mean, I did save your life. I'm totally yours; I've always been, just say the word," Li-Chun said, getting up and walking over to him. She sat on the bed and rubbed his arm.

D - "I need a partner for emotional needs, and I need a ride or die, literally. When it's the right time, I'll tell you why these cultists are trying to kill us. Can you—?" Dante was cut off by an eager Li-Chun.

LC - "Yes, I would love to be your ride or die." Li-Chun leaned over and kissed him. "Now, let's get some sleep and get ready for tomorrow."

She went to the couch, smiling as he stared back at her. His pistol with the silencer on it was on the bed by him. Her face was flushed as she got comfortable on the sofa.

LC - "So, what was in those syringes you shot in the Mercury Order and the Captain?" Li-Chun asked.

D - "Those syringes were filled with an experimental virus that will kill them in three days if they don't get the antidote. I have a nice plan to get some stolen items back or he can play tough and die. Tomorrow you and I will talk to him," Dante said, wincing in pain, making her get up quickly, rushing to check up on him.

He smiled and she gasped, mad that he tricked her.

LC - "Why would you scare me like that?" Li-Chun asked, angrily at him.

D - "It was just a joke. I haven't had a pretty nurse in years," Dante said.

Scene 29 (Dangerous in Love)

{The Next Day}

Dante and Li-Chun were dressed nicely; he was in a suit and Li-Chun had on a knee-length skirt and silk blouse, a colorful one. They were at an upscale cafe in the Diamond District, far away from criminal elements in the Redlight District. They had the laptop with them and since Dante knew the owner of the upscale cafe and used to help him out back in the day, they had the best table in the cafe.

He held out her chair for her and got her seated before he sat down, giving her a soft, sweet message in her ear and kissing her cheek. They ordered expresso and donuts that morning and were being extra flirty with each other. Not worrying about the dangerous situation ahead of them. They were armed and ready to fight, but just enjoyed their free time.

Dante was still injured, but his bulletproof vest gave him some support and a little comfort to his bruised ribs. Li-Chun put a little make up on him to hide the bruises from his fight with the Red Mercury and motorcycle crash. They used the phone Dante took off the captain after he was shot to call him on another secure line. They called the number, and he picked up, sounding sick. Dante kept his voice soft and calm as to not draw attention to the two of them in the packed cafe.

> D - "You sound sick, Captain Monroe; so sad. But listen, I can help you. Give me the briefcase and promise to stop sending hitmen after my friends and family, and I won't go after yours," Dante proposed.

> CM - "Deal, whatever you want. Just make this virus you've injected me with me go away. You're a sick man to resort to these tactics. I thought you wouldn't stoop that low," Captain Monroe said, coughing and hacking.

> D - "You can insult me all you want; you know what I want. That briefcase. In two days from now, the virus will kill the host. So, you'll have two days to show up and get the antidote or else kick the bucket," Dante said, calmly sipping his hot beverage.

CM - "I'm glad you think this is funny. I agree to your terms;
I don't want to die," Captain Monroe said.

D - "Okay, in the meanwhile, just wait for a call from us in a
few hours. Don't get too sick and die before then, okay, sir?
Thank you, eat some soup. Bye," Dante teased, hanging up.

Li-Chun was looking around the cafe and keeping an eye out for any kind of strange activity. She was a little afraid of him after his conversation with the captain. Dante was ruthless. He took her to the botanical gardens that morning. Afterwards, he walked her through the white and pink bed of leaves from the cherry blossom trees.

D - "I talked to the squad at the bunker, and everyone is fine;
they've been keeping busy. I brought you here because this
is a beautiful place, and you're beautiful to me. After all of
these years of knowing you, I like the woman you've become," Dante said, holding her hand.

LC - "Thanks. But it only builds to the excitement; I've been
waiting for this for years. But we have to remember our mission is bigger than us, as you tell me. All I ask is that you don't
lie to me," Li-Chun asked, looking at the flowers.

Scene 30 (Teach Me)

Mary was on the I.G.L.A. Starship in her living quarters. She was sitting on her bed and going through her Terminal on her wrist. She was amazed by the super advanced tech. She called Titan who was working on a device she knew nothing about or how it worked.

Titan answered and Mary was in a moment of shock, as she realized that she was basically Face Timing an intelligent gorilla on a planet-sized Starship, via Hologram Communication. If only her siblings knew that she has, in a short period of time, met Humans from the past and intelligent gorillas who were the masters of their destroyed planet. That had the Humans beings as the animals. A twist on life, completely different from what they've known.

T - "Are you alright, little one?" Titan asked. "I know this is overwhelming this first time around; it was for me," Titan said, tinkering with his gear.

M - "Really? You mean that you were nervous and a little afraid when you first arrived on the I.G.L.A. Starship? As massive as you are?" Mary asked.
Just then a 3D holographic model of a planet and its moons appeared in the middle of the room, and she quickly got up.

T - "Yes, little human, and it was very nerve-wracking. Because on Triton we were always aware of the UFOs that buzzed around. But we didn't have irrefutable proof, like your species. So, to be onboard this Starship and know the truth is nerve-wrecking. It only gets weird and strange from here on out. Mother has chosen me to be your Guardian and guide," Titan said.

T - "As you see on that Projection Map, the planet is called Sirux B; it's a Gas Giant. I'm going to be covering a few tools we're going to need on this journey of ours," Titan said.

M - "What, I just got here. Are you sure I'm qualified to be going on a mission to Sirux B or any planet, Titan?" Mary asked, a little nervous about going to a gas planet. "I just found out the Galaxy is crawling with life, and you want me to go on the planet and do what exactly?" Mary asked, interacting with the planet's Hologram.

T - "You will be fine. We will send a Scout Satelite ahead of our journey to the distress signal to gather intel. You're expected to do what you did so good back on your home planet," Titan said. He put his tools down and ate a banana.

M - "You want me to be a Space Investigative journalist I assume, huh? Solve the strange mysteries of the species of many worlds?" Mary asked, sarcastically.

T - "Exactly. You surely have the certain characteristics we need. I'm going to send an invite to my private Portal. It'll take you to the Terminal station to meet Muhammed and Afeni; we'll brief you then. So, please, get ready because you'll be in that suit for a while," Titan said.

M - "Okay, Titan, if you say so. Give me one Earth hour, and I'll be ready; my stomach is upset," Mary said.

Scene 31 (Planetary Investigator)

Mary was in the bathroom of her very interactive living quarters. As she sat on the toilet, a message about her body shown up in her field of vision. She realized that she took her suit off but forgot to take her helmet off. So, she saw her vitals in her vision. She read them, indicating her overall health and could even see her pulse. So, she left it on her head and used the bathroom.

She made the helmet disappear by using the Terminal. She took it off her wrist as she used the bathroom. She took a shower and put her lightweight suit on.

She accessed her terminal after she got dressed; her hair and body instantly dried as she left the shower. She didn't have her hair braided, so her afro was big, swaying as she moved around. She put her helmet on by the press of a button, and its fit was light, and she loved how simple it was to interact with the suit. She opened the Portal section on her Terminal, which could operate by thought alone. But she still used the manual way as Mother shown her.

The Portal opened up and she just looked at it for twenty minutes, thinking about the science behind the Portals and how easy they were to produce. The Portal looked like a six-foot-diameter Blackhole. It was something she had seen a lot in movies. It was something special and boring simultaneously. It was boring because the Portal was not big in size; it was her height and made no sound. She went through it anyway and ended up in an all-white room and saw the massive Titan in his I.G.L.A. Suit, which was silver and dark yellow.

> T - "Hello, Miss Mary. Welcome to the Void. This room is for testing Terminal systems. Some things are getting un-locked for your mission; take your helmet off. So, you can put this Terminal Chip on your temple," Titan instructed.

He walked over on two legs for a short period of time, because he had to focus on holding the Chip delicately on one of his huge fingers. Mary smiled when he waddled over, wearing a big spacesuit like hers, his big muscles showing through the suit.

> M - "I'm sorry, but I saw that look on your face. You hate walking like a Human, don't you?" Mary asked. "I'm not try-ing to insult you, Titan. You may be a different ape species

than me, but our facial features are too similar. We're related by a slim DNA percentage," Mary said.

T - "And that keen observation is why you're here, Mary. Now, once you put it against your temple, it will show the Terminal like a projection. Now you can access the Terminal with your mind. Some things will occur just with a thought. We will practice on a few things that require concentration," Titan said.

M - "Oh, my gosh, this is so cool," Mary said, getting a digital layout like a First-Person Shooter videogame in her eyesight as she put her helmet back on. "Wait, I feel like this is a crazy question, but can I fly?" Mary asked, freaking out at the highly advanced technology.

Scene 32 (With Power Comes Prowess)

T - "Yes, you can bend and manipulate the fabric of gravity
and time; you also can fly. You just have to access the gravity
section, and it will guide you through it," Titan said.

Mary did just that. Her head moved and so did her eyes as she used the
Thought Terminal. It felt like virtual reality games she experienced back home,
so she liked the feeling. She started to float, slowly gliding off the ground and
across the white room, coming back down on the ground in front of Titan,
who was fascinated with the small human.

T - "Fun, huh? Okay, next think of a Portal. And if you put
the Portal above you, you would have to then access the
Gravity Section to fly up into the Portal. Or fly down into
the Portal," Titan taught. "Just pick the portal type and destination in the Portal Section."

She took five minutes and went through the Portal Section of the Thought
Terminal and set up a tutorial that showed her how to set up Private, Planetary,
or I.G.L.A. Portals.

T - "Okay, good. Now, first weapon you get will be the time-
stun, and it is non-lethal weapon. Its purpose is to manipulate
the fabric of time and space," Titan said.

She did a mental example using the Thought chip and got a good feeling of
the time and gravity-based attack that was in the non-lethal category. She ac-
cidently froze Titan, quickly releasing him. He looked at her with his head
tilted slightly, looking annoyed.

M - "I'm sorry, Titan. I apparently have a lock-on system.
Did it hurt you?" Mary asked, embarrassed at her mistake.

T - "No. But next time, be very careful in how you load your weapon and don't forget that pointing your arm and fingers is a good way to be sure of your aim, as well as controlling your thoughts," Titan said, slowly lifting one of his fingers. Mary started to levitate and thought it was cool how he moved her around.

He produced a Portal. The two of them walked through it, and ended up in another white room, this time it was full of alien tech. Two tall, skinny, and majestic-looking Africans from her Earth joined them from a different time period. The two of them put down their tools and special glasses to greet them. Mary thought the man was handsome and found herself staring at him as he walked over. His female counterpart caught him smiling too hard at the new member.

A - "Hello, Mary. Welcome to one of our Terminal workshops. We've been expecting you; some of us more than others. Muhammad, stop drooling," Afeni said, with a hint of jealousy,

MD - "I'm sorry, Afeni. I mean, she is very pretty. The 3D Projection did not do you justice, but let's stick to the mission. Now, if you noticed, all of our long hair members have their hair braided. I made this Terminal app just for you," Muhammad said, holding her hand, too long for Afeni.

M - "Okay, what is it? Does it braid my hair, hands-free?" Mary asked.

Scene 33 (Mission: Syrux B)

MD - "Well, it does your hair into any protective style you can possibly imagine. And I know you think: Why is this important? Because your helmet that comes with your I.G.L.A. Spacesuit uses a Forcefield Technology that is invisible yet protective and there will be times you'll have to wear a metallic, physical helmet and one of those times will be coming up. Plus, it keeps critters from hiding in your Hair," Muhammad said, still holding her hand, too long for Afeni.

A - "And that mission of yours today will be sending you to a gas planet, and you will wear a mechanical Exo-suit on top of your existing suit, and the Exo-suit will take the gas from the surroundings and convert it into oxygen," Afeni said. "And if we see something that you could use, we will send it to you via Portal and it will go directly to your suit," Afeni said.

M - "I'm wondering if this will be a dangerous mission because I still haven't got a clue on what these alien creatures even look like. Are they hostile?" Mary asked as Titan sat down on the ground.

A - "That will be explained later in your briefing by the Support Team. But first, let's get you into your new Exo-suit; Titan you, too. We have to make sure it fits your big frame perfectly," Afeni said.

Muhammad guided her with his hand on her back to the suit which was standing up by itself. The suit looked like carbon fiber and was thicker than the normal Spacesuit. She went close to it, and it faded from view completely within a few steps. Mary instinctively looked down at her torso, and her suit looked darker but felt the same.

M - "Let me guess. The suit put itself on," Mary stated matter-of-factly.

A - "It's compatible with your current suit, and I had pro-grammed it to use your Terminal's' Gravity function to put quickly disassemble and reassemble on your body, giving you a tight fit and saving precious time," Afeni said.

MD - "We are here to help with your Terminal. We are the Department for Primate Terminal Support," Muhammad said.

A - "And we are here for support only, not to be so flirty," Afeni said, giving Muhammad a serious look.

Mary felt a little awkward, but Titan broke the tension as he stood up to keep the mission on time. He thanked the two, then opened up another Portal and they went through it to end up in the busy Astro-Pod and spacecraft dock. There were a lot of differently sized spacecraft that were shaped like the UFOs she saw back on her Earth. The Dock had had a huge forcefield window that Ships and Pods flew through into the blackness of space.

They went to an Astro-Pod that was like a medium-sized private jet, except it was wing and tail-less, shaped like a cigar, floating above the Dock's ground.

M - "Wow. This place is cool as hell!" Mary said.

The huge forcefield window that the Pods flew through had stars in the back-ground and even a small moon that her Terminal's live data feed said was only three hundred thousand miles away. The Starship had its own moon; Mary didn't know if it was artificial or a natural satellite.

Scene 34 (Mary's Home Away from Home)

M - "Wow, Titan, this is a Spacecraft of some kind, right? Because it looks like a UFO we see on Earth," Mary asked.

T - "Yes. They are means of transportation and also a personal Travel-Pod to different celestial bodies, whether on missions or approved travel. This Pod is yours to name, customize, and make yours to do as you see fit," Titan said.

M - "This is so cool!" Mary exclaimed. She walked to the private jet-sized Space-Craft that could fit Titan.

The Pod had a projection pop up for Mary to type the name of her Pod and choose a color theme. Mary chose dark pink and named the Ship *Curiosity*. The color changed before she even looked at it and she loved the outside color, which she thought in her mind how she wanted it to look, and it turned out that way.

The ship reminded her a lot of the *Star Wars* Space-Craft and the inside wasn't the white color that much of the I.G.L.A. was, but instead a gray color. White smoke shot through the doors as she entered. She assumed that the smoke from the main lobby was to sanitize her, as well as sterilize the Pod.

T - "Okay, this is the lobby of *Curiosity*. That whole left side is for plant and seed incubation, with a fully functional climate-controlled storage locker," Titan pointed out. "Right there in the middle is our Teleport Station and also a cargo port if we request things from the Planetary Star-Ship."

T - "On the other side is our Suit and Technology Storage. As you travel to the unlimited planetary destinations, you'll have to have suits and tech. that will help protect you out in the harsh atmospheres and climates. The next section of the Ship is the Living Quaters and it's just like your Living-Quaters on the I.G.L.A. Planetary Ship. Now, before we advance to the cockpit, do you have any questions?" Titan asked.

M - "Hell, yeah. Okay, if I have a plant growing station is that to survive or just to take my favorite plant from an alien planet and have my own supply? Is there ever going to be a situation in that I'm light years away from the support of the I.G.L.A. and have to survive with just our Suits and this growing pod alone?" Mary asked.

T - "Yes. On our later and most dangerous missions we're going to be eating what we've grown in our Plant Growing Station and yes, there will be times that we are light years away from the Ship and will have to use our knowledge and wit to make it back safely," Titan said.

M - "I need to see my family. When can I go back to my planet and see my siblings?" Mary asked.

T - "You will have a pass after the mission. I will personally see to it that you have a chance to go back," Titan reassured her. "But first, let's finish our tour and stay on track. You will see them, but I don't know if they will be able to comprehend what you've been through," Titan said.

M - "They know that there is life off Earth, they know our secret. Actually, many people know, they just don't have con-firmation," Mary said.

Titan took Mary through the lobby and through another passage way, it was a moving door this time and white smoke came through just as quickly as the doors opened and shut behind them. They checked their rooms, and they were both surprised to see how many small personal items they had in their Living Quarters. They left, heading towards to the cockpit and Mary was fascinated by the screens and the whole setup of the Astro-Pod. The screens were huge and covered the floor to the ceiling, with two cockpits that were futuristic. It looked like nothing she was used to.

Mary sat in the smaller seat she assumed to be her seat, since Titan was a huge, framed primate. That made her feel secure because he was on her side. Titan sat down on his pad, he didn't have a seat, because lotus style of sitting was his favorite. Titan sometimes liked to levitate with the help of his Terminal and suit. Mary was freaked out the first time she saw the huge gorilla floating in his Outdoor Living-Quarters back on the Starship.

M - "Okay, this is so f****ing cool. But I don't know how to drive one of these Pods. Do you know how, sir?" Mary asked, not touching anything, but loving the see-through, inter-active window, which showed the space in front of them while giving a live-data stream of everything inside of the Astro-Pod and Space-Craft Dock.

T - "Yes. I know how to operate the Pod, if you access your Terminal with your Thought Chip, you can use the Terminal to teach you how to fly properly. But until then, I'll fly for a while," Titan instructed his Captain.

M - "Cool. I guess I'll just get my training lessons in while we fly there. I'm looking at how far Sirux-B is, and my Hel-met Interface says seven days. What? No way," Mary said.

T - "I can use our Portal function on the Pod and fly through Portals. It's a limit on how far we can travel via Portal, so I'll have to use that technique repeatedly," Titan said.

She looked at the asteroids flying by, as well as the planets and stars. She was amazed at the many different colors and gases there were in space.

M - "I wish Beccah and Dante could see this. They wouldn't believe all this. And to top it off, I'm working with a gorilla that is from an alternate Earth, where the apes rule over the humans," Mary said. "So, are you married, do you have a partner on the I.G.L.A., or am I being too nosey?"

T - "I had a wife a long time ago, in a different life. She was killed when our planet was destroyed," Titan said, in a sad tone.

M - "That's sad. I'm sorry to hear that," Mary said.

T - "Don't be, just think your mission now is preventing this from happening to other lifeforms. And my job is to assist you, Captain Mary," Titan said.

Mary was walking through the Pod, checking out the silver and darkly colored Pod interior. She spent her time on her Terminal, getting familiar with the functions, such as levitating and using Portals. She used the Portals to bypass using the mechanical doors, that automatically folded when she was about to walk through them. Titan was in his room getting some sleep, and Mary sat there in the cockpit and just watched the various planets as the Pod traveled by them, not succumbing to the gravitational pull of the spectacular planets.

The Pod had Portals surrounding it and asteroids and other space debris was redirected as they passed through an asteroid belt, moving towards the edge of the Milky Way Galaxy. Mary found that both heart-racing and cool at the same time. She got up and floated around the Pod checking it out when she got an incoming Hologram Projection request and she accepted it. Holding her arm up and horizontally, so the projection could be right next to her face, like a Face-time call.

> M - "Mother, it's nice to see you. How are you doing?" Mary asked, so excited to talk to another Human. "I feel like that look means I'm getting briefed about something serious," Mary said, relaxing in her chair, embracing her new, dream-like reality.

> MA - "You are indeed in due for a briefing about the life forms who sent the distress frequency. I've been monitoring your travel progress; you are at least a day away from entering their Galaxy," Mother's hologram stated. Her image was replaced by an image of the ghost-like creatures.

They looked like ghosts with two glowing red eyes. They were at least four feet tall, and Mary was looking at their bio and information. They lived in domes like small huts, and Mary was trying to take it all in. She knew it was going to get weird. That next Projection came out side by side and the small, red, one-foot creatures, made her think of lobsters.

MA - "Okay, so the ghost like creature with the glowing red eyes is the Reux and the small, red shelled life form is called the Zenon. The Reux has found a way to use the Methane gas to form a protective cloak around their fragile bodies to protect them against harsh, extreme heat. The Zenon species have a very intricate outer shell, that is surprisingly leak-proof and very durable. They are your first traditional Alien encounter, this is very normal to us on the I.G.L.A., we have many gas based and shelled covered life forms onboard," Mother's Projection said.

M - "Okay, so I use the Pod to review the Intel you have given me, then we respond to the signal, which will become clear as we get closer to their planet and multi-moon satellites?" Mary asked.

MA - "Yes, my beautiful, black cosmic daughter. The signal will become clear, and you will be able to communicate with the E.T.s sending out the signal. But this is the basic overview of their organic and ghastly makeup. Your mission is to help save them and prevent the planet from being destroyed by the Star Killers. Remember to check for plant life, they will be very different from Earth plants," Mother informed.

M - "Yes, Mother, I will do my best. Titan and I are on the job," Mary said.

Scene 37 (Before the Meet and Greet)

Dante and Li-Chun were safely back at the safe house/bunker in New Brington. Dante had a lot of bruises and even a limp, everyone was concerned about him. Especially Beccah, who rushed to his side as soon as he got in the lounge area of the bunker from his mission with Li-Chun.

They had the T.V. on the news, and they knew he was the man on the crazy motorcycle stunt/escape through the Red-Light District. That incident was reportedly how the RLDPD Captain was injured, according to the *Freedom Journal*.

Dante eased down on the couch, surrounded Beccah, Pam, Fatman and little Frank, who had on headphones to not hear the convo between the adults. Li-Chun and Beccah were on opposites sides of Dante as he sat.

D - "Alright. We are on the list of targets for the Mercury Order. They want us all dead. We have a strong chance at their organization, to kill them first. I've got some things lined up to level the playing field for us. It's gonna take all of us doing what we do best, don't be afraid or nervous. I'm actually glad that I'm leading you guys through this because you guys are really strong and resilient," Dante said, getting a round of applause from Li-Chun, who was trying to be supportive as she could. "Yep, and while we were doing our mission, we kinda had a heart to heart. We're going to try to be a little closer. I'd rather not be alone on this journey," Dante said.

LC - "This is a good sign, that even though we are fighting the good fight, love can blossom," Li-Chun said, kissing his bruised cheek.

D - "Okay, let's take today and call our schools and jobs to make up whatever excuse works, use your sick days and be careful. Beccah you can use the satellite phone to call Trixie. Nobody leaves, we are officially off of the grid for a while," Dante instructed.

Dante and Li-Chun were alone in the master bedroom above the bunker. He was taking off his shoes, sitting on the edge of the bed. Li-Chun was in her silk Kimono, with a small .38 strapped to her ankle and for some strange reason that turned Dante on. Li-Chun was standing up watching the T.V. monitor to check the perimeter of the house. Dante came and wrapped his arms around her waist, making her smile.

LC - "Is that your—?" Li-Chun asked, he cut her off.

D - "Oh, sh**, my bad, that's my gun. I usually sleep with one," Dante said, removing it, sitting it on the dresser, pulling her closer again.

LC - "Okay, that's not a gun I feel this time," Li-Chun said.

D - "It's not a gun, but it'll still go off," Dante said, kissing the back of her neck.

One day left on the deadline for the swap, the vaccine for the briefcase containing Alien technology. It was to keep the captain of the RLDPD alive, so he has no choice but to accept the deal. Everyone was inside of the bunker, underneath the house in the bunker's main lobby area. They were sitting on comfy leather couches with four, eighty-two-inch T.V.s mounted on the wall, showing many different channels, as well as the news. Dante was on the phone, and Li-Chun was studying their huge map of the Red-Light District.

Rebeccah was talking to Trixie on the satellite phone, while picking out her afro. Trixie knew what was going on in regards to knowing about Aliens and the Mercury Order and her best friends near assassination. But Beccah just wanted to talk about SOPA gossip and their band. They talked for hours. Trixie was in school but had one of her Air Pods in and talked quietly.

Fatman and his family were getting along and were connecting with each other. Li-Chun was quiet and angry at the people that tried to kill them, she had a look on her face. She wanted to spar with one of the mercs. She convinced one of them and everybody watched as they got in stance, taking off their weapons. He had a cocky smirk on his face, thinking he was going to take a few of her jabs, letting her release steam. Dante watched, he worried the Merc would hurt her, because he chose only dangerous, ex-military mercenaries.

D - "Don't underestimate her and don't try to knock her head off, either," Dante said. The Merc was too confident in his skills.

LC - "He can't touch me, sweetie," Li-Chun said.

They moved around feeling each other out and the Merc saw her foot work and knew she was a fighter. That made him throw a punch. Li-Chun leaned back, missing her nose by inches. She used his momentum to make him spin around with his back to her. She quickly kicked him in the back of his knees, with two quick kicks making him fall to his knees. Li-Chun flipped over him, holding onto his shoulders. Taking a step back, she went through the full motion of a kick, but stopped with the bottom of her foot stopping right in front of his face. She bowed and helped him up as her friends and the other Mercs applauded at her display of martial arts.

R - "You have to teach me that; that was too acrobatic," Beccah said.

Later on that day, Dante, Fatman, and a squad of his mercs were in the war
room. The room had a huge screen on the wall, showing the blueprints of a
building. He called Captain Monroe; they had the technology to trace the call,
but Dante wanted to know his true location, just in case. The captain answered
the call and Fatman smiled.

D - "Meet us at the jewelry store in the Diamond District
and come alone or die from sickness. And if you did anything
to the contents of the briefcase I promise, I will inject this
virus into your family," Dante said.

Scene 39 (A Lost Terminal Part 2)

Dante and Fatman took off in the Beast and quickly sped towards the Diamond District. He had the captain give them immunity as they ran redlights and broke traffic violations. Dante had his mercs posted up in the jewelry store and on top of the stores owned by their partners and money launderer, Goldstein.

They arrived to see a skinny and sick-looking captain, coughing and looking close to dying. He quickly gave Dante the briefcase, not wasting time. Dante opened the small briefcase to see what appeared to be a watch. It was a Terminal Super Watch from the I.G.L.A. and Dante knew it had to be real alien technology, even if it looked like a smartphone mixed with a bracelet.

He closed the briefcase. He had a real nurse earn some extra money by administering the IV bag and the needle in the captain's arm. Dante left him as soon as he shut the briefcase, he didn't say too much during the exchange. They got back in the Beast and had two GMC SUVs to provide back up, for a worst-case scenario. They took a shortcut to New Brington.

Beccah snuck out of the bunker and met up with Trixie. The two of them sat at their favorite pizza parlor, and they ate good, hot pizza and watched Sports on the T.V. Beccah had a pistol with a silencer on it in her purse; she also had a smoke grenade and flash bang.

She was ready to run, knowing all of the hidden paths and alleys,

> T - "So, how long are you going to be out of sight? Because you know I don't have that many friends," Trixie said. Beccah frowned.

> R - "You have a few friends. I'll be only be gone for a week. I'm out on a family emergency if anyone asks," Beccah said, chomping on pizza. "I'll miss you. But remember, this thing is huge and I'm kinda happy it's happening to us."

> T - "You're happy that a cult has you on its hit list? What kinda gun are you packing?" Trixie asked with excitement.

Beccah let her peek in her backpack, which was bulletproof but stylish and fashionable. She saw the pistol with the silencer and flashlight/laser combo that was attached to the bottom. Her mouth dropped when she saw the grenades, one had a blue pin and the other had an orange pin.

> T - "Wow. You ain't nothing to f*** with. I thought that revolver was something," Trixie said, choking up. She started to cry and was emotional, which is rare for her.

Beccah got up and went around the table, inside of their booth and gave Trixie a hug, taking a bite of her pizza.

> R - "I know, please stop crying before I start crying," Rebeccah said, rubbing her back.

Later on that evening, Beccah arrived back at the bunker, making sure she wasn't being followed. The coast seemed clear.

Fatman sent Pam and his son to Alabama to stay with his grandparents, whom he trusted. They were tough country people with guns and survival knowledge. He sent two of his best people to watch over them.

He and Dante arrived back at the bunker with the suitcase in their possession. Beccah made it back before him and was very smooth in her sneakiness. She went over to Dante, who sat the briefcase down, calling everyone to a huddle, as he sat down. Everyone was ready to hear what information he had to share.

Dante took out the Terminal, it was the size of a bracelet that had a long touchscreen and holographic capabilities. The Terminal lit up as he put it on his wrist. It pricked his skin to draw some blood.

LC - "You poisoned the captain to get your hands on this technology; it looks cool. What is it, exactly?" Li-Chun asked.

D - "This is alien tech; my sister has one. She can apparently do some crazy things with it," Dante said.

B - "Is it in Human language? Can we use it?" Beccah asked, as the Terminal accepted his blood.

LC - "What can it do?" Li-Chun asked, looking over his shoulder.
Dante played with it for a while, focusing on the Terminal.

D - "Well, it's written in English, so I can understand something," Dante said. "Here's a message from the last user."

Dante was shocked when the message turned out to be a hologram of what appears to be a talking, intelligent chimp in a Space-Suit. The chimp was talking with proper English.

H? - "If you're seeing this, I don't have my Terminal and that means I'm in danger," the chimp said. "But the mission remains, recover our stolen technology. Earth cannot advance that quickly. The Humans will destroy the planet," the Chimp said, showing him how to use the basic functions of the Terminal. "If you are using the Terminal, you are related to me in some kind of way or fashion. The planet or date doesn't matter, secure the three artifacts, and return them to the I.G.L.A. Starship," the hologram ended.

Dante, Li-Chun, Beccah, and Fatman were open-mouthed and stunned at the shocking revelation. There was so much to take in. One of the items was showing up on a world map Hologram on the terminal on Dante's wrist. Just then the house shook as red, flashing alerts went off in the bunker. They checked the monitors only to see a tank with a tall, brunette woman in a red dress sitting elegantly on top of the tank.

D - "Everybody retreat, get the f*** out now!" Dante yelled to his mercs. "Use the subway tunnels; shoot to kill!"

R - "That thing can teleport us out of here, we should use it," Beccah said as the tank kept shooting, destroying the house.

Scene 41 (Touchdown)

Mary and Titan were onboard her Ship *Curiosity*, using the Pod's two living quarters to suit up for their landing on the surface of Sirux-B. The pod stayed five hundred thousand feet above the thick, toxic atmosphere but close enough to use the gravitational pull of the large gas planet as an anchor.

Mary was not afraid as she put her I.G.L.A. Suit on and then her Exo-suit, made for gas planets and extreme conditions. The suit was mechanical, with metal parts and plastic. The helmet wasn't made from the invisible Force Field technology. Instead made of a strong plastic with metal components.

She met up with Titan in the main lobby. Titan sent a message to the Reux. The Reux were ghost-like, that looked like transparent octopus and had tentacles that helped them move through the methane-filled atmosphere. They got to the Teleportation Station and both stood on the platform, and it quickly teleported them.

She blinked and missed how quick the process of long-distance teleport travel was. She was absolutely blown away with the scene. The sky was purple, and all of the vegetation was black and thin, like spaghetti, wiggling and moving crazily.

The Reux creatures lived in pods that were also black, so they stood out against the light purple sky with red clouds. The creatures knew the two had arrived as one of the bigger Reux floated its way down with dozens following behind it. The creature was definitely fascinating, Mary thought as it floated towards them.

As the creatures approached, the leader was way bigger than Titan, who was a massive gorilla. The three moons were in the sky at the same time and it was a cool sight. Mary had her stream of info coming inside of her helmet for everything she was looking at.

> T - "Mary, stand still. Let them show us how they want to communicate, since they are friendly. Have you seen any organisms like this before?" Titan asked.

> M - "Yes. They look just like our octopus back home; they live under water. We can't communicate with them, though. Maybe we'll have something of a connection here," Mary stated, already in detective mode.

The big Reux leader came very close to them floating, its tentacles moving as if was they were propelling it through water. It extended one of its tentacles and sent off a spark of electricity and Mary remembered her training. Her helmet said the spark was not high in voltage, it was a safe transfer of data.

Mary didn't hesitate to extend her arm so that she could receive the data spark. It hit her mechanical hand and the Exo-suit started to process the spark. One second later, the info was available for them both, her suit was linked with Titan's. They both had access to each other's vitals and data.

M - "This is the Queen of the Species. They don't have names, apparently, that's irrelevant. But their title is the Reux, they produce this toxic chemical and before it shows us, it wants to know something," Mary said, reading exactly what was on her screen's FOV—field of view.

Scene 42 (Escape to Mexico Part 2)

With the bunker collapsing all around them in the New Brington Suburb, the woman on the tank was now eating an apple. Taunting them, sitting cross legged in her patent red leather dress. Beccah, Li-Chun, Fatman, and Dante were all hunkered down together. Dust and wood falling on top of them, blinding them with smoke and ashes. The underground bunker was falling down with every massive tank round.

Dante used the Terminal to bring up a Portal. Everyone grabbed hands and walked through the circular Portal. In the blink of an eye, they were on an agave farm. Fatman sat there stunned, dusting off his clothes, checking to see if he had all of his limbs. Nothing but agave plants and lush vegetation could be seen for miles.

> R - "Where in the world are we, and I mean that literally? Where are we, Dante?" Rebeccah asked, her afro dirty.

> D - "It appears Mexico, by the looks of these blue agave. We are somewhere in South America. But, in the meantime, let's find somewhere to set up camp. Remember don't tell anyone about our mission. This is need to know," Dante instructed.

They walked until night time. Arriving at a farming village in what appeared to truly be Mexico, just by how the locals talked and looked. Li-Chun found a small hotel with no cars, just a few donkeys and a horse out front. Luckily, the hotel had a giftshop with clothes that fit them.

The guys easily decided that the two girls could get the bed and they would get the floor, they didn't care at all.

> R - "So, I'm just going to say this, and I know it may ruffle some feathers, but you got to admit, that brunette lady is badass. I mean she sat on the tank as it was firing, that was dope. She ate a f****** apple; that's a bad mofo," Beccah said.

> LC - "Well, don't like her too much, darling," Li-Chun said, braiding Beccah's big afro into braids, to hide her signature

look. "I'm going to kill her."

F - "I know. But that was badass, though. She has to be from the Mercury Order, with all that red on," Fatman said.

D - "More than likely. But for tonight we rest. I have my phone, and it's fully charged, so I'm gonna set us up while I have 100% battery. We all have our phones, even though this village has no real electric grid. We have lights and running water, so relax, and tomorrow we look for leads," Dante said. Li-Chun gave her spot to Dante, who was still recovering from his injury. She was starving and tired at the same time.

R - "Another thing I feel we should talk about is the fact that we successfully traveled through a Portal from a watch. If we could tell people what we just did, we could change humanity in a way it's not ready for. Like our Ape cousin said on the Terminal message, we really need to find the other alien tech pieces," Beccah said to them. Sitting in between Li-Chun's legs as she tried to tame her big afro.

Scene 43 (Zenon Phenom)

Mary and Titan were on the black, spaghetti-like grass of a huge black field. The vegetation got more interesting the further the two explored on the huge Exo-planet. But first, Mary had to communicate with the huge Reux leader. Mary used her Terminal to send a message back to the Reux leader.

M - "Has this planet ever been visited by beings that are like us? We are primates; we live in a Galaxy one light year away," Mary said. She even sent an image of Earth and a few primates that she could think of, and her thoughts were translated into the Terminal.

RL - "The Reux Pre-date Sirux-B. Over this planet's history, we have seen an untold number of variations of life. And throughout the span of this planet, I've seen many variations of Primates, in many different dimensions and on many different planes of reality," the Reux leader communicated via Electric Conscience Transmission.

Mary wanted to press the big Reux further about Humans from her home planet but thought that wasn't her mission. Everything she was seeing was being fed directly back to the I.G.L.A Planetary Starship, Mother could be watching. So, she kept it professional.

M - "Tell us about the threat to your species and what we can do to help the Reux continue to exist?" Mary asked, sending out an Elec-Comms to the big Reux.

RL - "The Zenon are of recent creation. Their origins are from the moon Zerux. Foreign species are controlling them. They are using a high pitch frequency to control them. Stop the foreign species from manipulating the Zenon. They are naturally peaceful and easy to be influenced. If the Zenon continue to be used by the foreign species, then this planet will be on a course to self-destruction. The Zenon are destroying the atmosphere with their actions," the Reux leader communicated.

Mary and Titan let the Reux return to their Pods that floated in the purple sky. The two of them accessed a Portal and was sent back to Lobby of Mary's Ship *Curiosity*. Mary took off the Exo-suit's helmet and she stood there for a minute. Just sitting there staring at the planet's info being projected mid-air.

She walked to the Projection and used two fingers to stretch the planet and make a 3D projected image that she could manipulate with her hand, like an actual golf ball-sized ball. Titan sat down and used the Portal to bring him a bunch of bananas, offering Mary a couple of them, which she happily accepted.

M - "Okay, so I'll need to get some sleep before I make any announcements or say my ideas. I need to think about all of this. I mean, I went from not knowing if aliens even existed to Planetary Detective in a week," Mary said, yawning.

T - "I understand. Remember, you are the captain of this vessel. I go as you order me to, Captain Mary. I respect your judgement, you were chosen to be here," Titan said, munching on the fruit.

Scene 44 (Jungles and the Bottomless Pit)

{Dante, Rebeccah, Fatman, and Li-Chun}

The four of them were on horseback following their guide across the Mexican countryside to meet Dante's South American connect. Dante managed to find a nice place for them to sleep on their third night in the Mexico wilderness. Camping out under the moon and stars. It was cool as they slept. Slowly trekking along behind their escort, who rode a donkey, early that next morning.

> R - "So, what's the plan boss, where are we going?" Beccah asked. She had on a big hat to block the sun and a long sleeve shirt.

> D - "We are going to meet my contact up in a farming town called Lareno. They have a nice market. We will look for one of the artifacts from there, the Terminal says to come here. We will get some weapons, as we are not the only ones looking for the artifacts," Dante said.

They crossed a river on the horses. Taking in the scenery, amazed by the jungle they were going through, on the trail. They spent four hours on the trail, seeing all of the breathtaking landscape, until they arrived in the bustling and thriving agave and marijuana farming town. The marijuana and agave came with armed Cartel members.

They put their horses in a stable, since horses and horse drawn carts were the go-to means of transportation. Lareno has electricity, but few cars and motorcycles. They went inside of the bar and sat down at a table ordering some food and drinks.

Scene 45 (Jungles and the Bottomless Pit)

A white man in a suit came up to their table and handed Dante some keys and an envelope. He said few words, Dante trusted him. Seeing another American was refreshing, even if it was a firearm and drug struggling CIA agent. The agent left him some tactical equipment in a military Jeep, which made Li-Chun smile. After they ate in the bar, the team followed the agent throughout the village. A street vendor selling clothes in a Lareno market caught the groups attention. They spent the evening getting personal products for hygiene, along with some new clothes and hats.

Later on that night, the four of them sat around the dinner table in the modest Lareno home provided by Dante's connect. The girls cooked, using fresh veggies from the market. Li-Chun coached Beccah, considering her vast restaurant experience. They made chicken burritos and was surprised at how comfortable they were cooking on the open fire stovetop. They were are all laughing and having a good time. Even though they were forced to travel through a Portal, in desperation and under extreme tank fire.

> D - "Okay, guys. Tomorrow, we have to investigate the location on this map on my Terminal. It says we are very close by," Dante said, chewing on his food. He leaned over to whisper in Li-Chun's ear. "I love that dress you got from the vendor; it suits you," Dante whispered.

> F - "We still hear y'all. Don't hide your love now. We can't watch T.V. So, an action, romance, sci-fi movie will just be us right now. Tell her the chicken burritos were good. Women love cooking for their men," Fatman coached.

Dante thought why not? After all, they went through, a little P.D.A. wouldn't hurt.

Fatman was driving Rebeccah, Dante, and Li-Chun in a Jeep through the jungle to get to an ancient marvel, the Bottomless Pit. The Pit is circular in its design and is surrounded by lush vegetation in the dense jungle. How deep into the Earth it goes remains unknown, and no scientific instrument can measure the depth accurately.

The gift that Dante's contact provided was four tactical, bullet-proof vests, helmets, and weapons. They happily and hesitantly put the vests on, knowing they'd get into a gun battle at one point. Fatman continued to travel the path, Dante sat in the passenger side with an M-16 ready.

R - "Hey, guys, we have some company behind us. Can I start shooting now?" Beccah asked. She had on a vest that was half her small frame.

D - "Wait. Let's see if they are friendly first, make sure to aim your rifle downwards since it's fully automatic, it has a kick to it," Dante said, calm and alert.

Fatman kept driving, the trailing black Jeeps getting closer and closer. Li-Chun recognized the soldier's Mercury Order logos on their camo uniforms. She sat her M-16 on the window seal after rolling the window down. She grabbed the rifle tightly and looked at Dante, who was looking through a of pair binoculars. He had a duffle bag loaded with an unknown weapon. Beccah sat her gun on the window, as well as Li-Chun. Dante climbed up halfway through the sun-roof. He saw the Mercury Order logo and the soldiers attempting to aim their guns.

Dante started firing at the Jeep's front window, leaving a string of bullets across the windshield splattering blood everywhere on the inside. The enemy Jeep crashed into a tree and caught on fire. Dante stayed in position hanging out of the sunroof as a squad of Jeeps came roaring on the horizon. Dante smiled as a few bullets hit his vest.

D - "Drive, Fatman, drive!" Dante yelled, screaming loudly as he can. "Girls shoot, shoot," he yelled.

The sound of gunfire was deafening as everybody fired at the enemy Jeeps. Beccah and Li-Chun were shooting out of the back windows at the Jeeps as they sped through the narrow road in the Jungle.

They managed to take care of the vehicles by killing the drivers and that made the SUV's steer off course, crashing into the trees in a loud explosion. Dante shot the remaining soldiers that hung out their Jeeps before they were consumed in the flames. Dante ran out of rifle ammo; he quickly climbed back inside and went to the duffle bag. Fatman continued to speed down the path to the Pit in the Jungle's center.

D - "Y'all okay in here?" Dante asked. "Okay, cool, don't get too comfortable. We still have to fight. It's not over yet, load your clips up while we have time, check your ammo," Dante instructed. He pulled out a grenade launcher that had a six-teen-round revolver-like drum and Beccah smiled.

Li-Chun noticed Dante had caught a few rounds in the chest, luckily the vest caught it. She checked the rest of his body, as he held the grenade launcher.

D - "I'm fine, let's get ready for the next wave of them. They are well-funded and have military equipment and training, so shoot to kill," Dante said.

Fatman was driving fast as it started to rain, making the dirt road muddy. Mud flying everywhere made Dante chuckle. Hearing the engines of motorbikes and quads roaring through the foliage. He climbed back through the sunroof, this time with the grenade launcher as the quads got closer to the Jeep.

Beccah was shooting out of the side window at the soldiers on the motorbikes. One agent drove and the other sat on the back firing at their Jeep. Dante started firing the grenades at their bikes and sent them flying all over the Jungle into the tress and foliage, the motorbikes exploding in the mud. He the climbed back down after firing sixteen grenades at the quads and motorbikes. Rebeccah and Li-Chun were reloading their magazines. Beccah noticed Li-Chun bleeding from her arm, Dante quickly checked her out and treated her wound. She wasn't shot but grazed. Dante wrapped her cut up. Kissing Li-Chun's and Beccah's forehead. He went back to his seat and checked his duffle bag.

R - "Wow dude, how many guns do you have? Does this mean we have more Red Mercury soldiers to deal with?" Rebeccah asked, checking the GPS that Fatman was using, as he smoked a cigarette. "We only have five minutes left to the Pit."

D - "Okay, we're close. I think we will see the woman that wears the red dress. I have an idea; I think we can use the Terminal to get to the bottom of the Bottomless Pit, safely. I think that young woman is using Alien Tech, so kill her if you get the shot. Fatman, good f****** driving, everybody stay ready," Dante said, reloading the grenade launcher.

Dante pulled out a military-grade rocket launcher and projectiles. The projectiles were carried in a suitcase. He loaded a rocket in the launcher as the sound of the tank got closer, it was very loud. He fired off a rocket from the sunroof and it hit the front of the tank. As the smoke cleared, Dante loaded another round in the launcher and was surprised to see the woman. He fired the second round directly at the woman sitting on top the tank.

The caramel-colored woman held out her arm in front of her and the rocket stopped mid-air, everyone watched as the rocket disassembled. She made the metal turn into a heart and explode into a bigger heart, Fatman saw it in the rearview. Dante climbed back in the Jeep.

> LC - "Yep. Sure enough, she has alien tech. Brace yourselves; she's just toying with us," Li-Chun said.

Just as she said that the Jeep was slowing down, and the brakes didn't seem to work at all. They were quickly approaching the Bottomless Pit as the tank was gaining ground. The heavy rain made the Jeep stop fast because of the thick mud. Dante made everyone jump from the Jeep and fast. He jumped out, after everyone dived into the mud. The Jeep flew into the Pit. He pulled his mud-covered arm out of the ground and the Terminal was spotless and seemed to not get dirty at all. He accessed the Portal Menu on his Terminal watch and selected a Portal.

They saw the tank and tried their best to climb through the mud to the Portal to avoid a tank round. They touched the Portal and ended up in a black void.

> R - "Wow, this is cool. Are we in between dimensions right now? Dante, fix this please, even though it's cool," Beccah said, confused.

Scene 47 (The Sanctuary)

{Dante, Fatman, Li-Chun and Rebeccah}

They left the black void and it turned into a sanctuary, vast in size and total space. The background where the walls were supposed to be were a fading orange color, like a sunset. There were church-like pews and other furniture around. Beccah was nervous.

Dante looked at the Terminal on his wrist as the other three looked around in awe. Beccah was tugging on Dante's shirt and looking straight ahead. He stopped looking at his Terminal and followed her gaze to the woman in the red, patent leather dress. She was clapping as she approached them. She was a beautiful, tall, and bronze colored woman with long dreads that were braided together. She appeared to be in her late twenties.

> D - "Y'all, don't shoot or do anything drastic. She obviously is toying with us," Dante said. They were covered in mud, he sighed.

The woman walked a little closer and stopped a few feet in front of them. They were dirty and rough-looking.

> Z - "I'm Zalena. I'm the one who sent those agents to after you. I knew you would take care of them with no problem. You guys are extremely special, whether you believe it or not. But right now, you guys are in my home, and you're dropping mud everywhere. So, let's get you all cleaned up so we can talk," Zalena said, cheerfully smiling and sounding upbeat.

> LC - "How did you know we would kill those Red Mercury agents? Because Dante got hurt?" Li-Chun asked, taking a step closer to Zalena, not afraid of her. Dante gently pulls her back for protection since Zalena stopped a tank round just a few minutes ago.

Zalena was playing host in her underground sanctuary. She smiled as Dante calmed down Li-Chun. He made her take a step back and get behind him.

> D - "Baby, just relax, and let's hear what she has to say. She has unknown power; let's just observe for the moment," Dante whispered in her ear, as low as possible for only her to hear.

> Z - "Don't worry, I have no intentions of killing you. Luckily for you guys there's a bigger problem we need to address. But, out of respect for The Mercury Order Temple, you must clean yourselves and I have just the perfect place," Zalena said.

She produced a Portal and the four of them simultaneously voiced displeasure at the thought of going through one of her Portals.

> R - "I'm sorry, miss, but we've just been introduced. After you tried to kill us, so you have to understand our skepticism," Rebeccah said, her braided head all muddy.

> Z - "Okay. Dante, sir, type bathroom in your Terminal and it will take you to one from a recent location. There are a lot of bathrooms on the Terminal Multi-Dimension Interface," Zalena instructed.

Dante did exactly what she said, and he pulled up a Portal. Zalena was the first to walk through it, to show faith and everyone followed Dante's lead when he followed her. They were inside of a big bathroom only to find Zalena running hot water for them, complete with bubbles.

Scene 48 (Forbidden Knowledge)

Li-Chun and Dante let Rebeccah take her shower first as they all waited back in the sanctuary. Dante and Li-Chun took their shower together, taking turns washing each other. Zalena was still playing host.

They came out of the Portal after showering and put on some clean clothes. The sanctuary was a strange place, the walls were molten magma and flowed smoothly. The ceiling was just pitch black.

> R - "Wow, this is cool. Where are we? Are we back underground in the sanctuary?" Rebeccah asked. She didn't know what to make of Zalena. Dante had to tell Beccah to not get attached; she did try to kill them.

> Z - "No, ma'am. We are more than just underground; we are at the center of the Earth and this other worldly tech is the reason it's possible. I must admit. I know just the basic mechanics, but that's more than enough." Zalena smiled, her heels clicking as they approached a door that was just standing up with no frame or hinges, in the middle of the vast sanctuary.

> D - "So, what are we doing here? Are you friend or foe? You said we played a role in a bigger plot and didn't even know. So, when can you elaborate on that? We need to know where this is going," Dante asked, as she opened the door.

They looked through the door, which only shown the other side of the sanctuary as they glanced inside. The room they entered looked like a greenhouse with lush, brightly colored flowers, bright pottery, lawn chairs, and a small table with a pitcher of lemonade and some glasses. She motioned for them to sit down in the chairs. She poured everyone a glass, including herself, and was the first to drink to show it wasn't poisoned.

> LC - "Okay, let's hear it. You've had quite the introduction, Zalena said," Li-Chun said, legs crossed.

Z - "Yes, well, it's simple. I know you guys have been fighting and just trying to survive, which is all my fault, I'm sorry, I used you guys to have an unnecessary fight with the R.L.D.P.D. I owe Captain Monroe one," Zalena said, sipping her lemonade. "It's simple really, we have to continue our ancestors' work. Dante can use that Terminal because you are related to the previous owners. It's your/our job to get the remaining technology before they are put together and activated. We have to get them back, because if mankind reaches Star Killer status the I.G.L.A will appear before the planet and that won't end well," Zalena said.

FM - "So, the I.G.L.A must be some intergalactic Organization and our mission is to get their technology and secure it. So, they can retrieve it and save Humanity from destroying itself?" Fatman asked.

Z - "Yes, exactly the Intergalactic Liaison Allegiance, that's where Mary is. She is a part of the I.G.L.A. They have been here before Man evolved. Over time, Primates earned key positions on the super alien team," Zalena said. "They don't want humanity to know about life on other planets. It would halt our growth as a species and cause our downfall," Zalena said.

Scene 49 (Connecting Dots)

Zalena was filling them in on some real heavy details. Rebeccah was listening and taking notes on a notepad, that was brought in via Portal by Zalena at Beccah's request. As they sat amongst the flowers in the greenhouse, they were still in the Earth's core.

D - "Okay, so what is it that kept us alive. You did send a tank and an army to kill us?" Dante asked.

Z - "Well, I really never had your lives in that much danger. Everything was real, but I did put an Anti-Matter shield around you guys, you were okay. I'm sorry, I was wrong to do that. I hope I can regain your trust; I'm just a fan of human action movies," Zalena said.

R - "Wait, are you not Human? Because you said that as if you're not of the same primate species?" Beccah asked, thinking about her recent school lesson on the many different hominids that existed.

Z - "I am Human. But there is an infinite and diverse array of intelligent life. I've seen Alien action movies and they are very weird," Zalena said. "But we are not talking about that right now, we are talking about our shared mission," Zalena said.

R - "What is our next step, Zalena? Wait." Beccah had a light bulb go off in her head. "Zalena is an Exo-planet we discovered recently. What are your ties to that the Exo-planet?" Rebeccah asked.

Z - "That kind of awareness and Planetary knowledge is why you've been chosen to save humanity from itself and keep the natural order going. I was named that by my parents, you have the chance to ask them that. Now, the sanctuary has a Portal to the first artifact. I'm unable to access it though. It's locked by a genetic code in the terminal, and it unlocks the another one, the Time Portal," Zalena said.

R - "Let me guess… Dante and I are the two bloodline relatives that can access the Time Portal?" Beccah asked, eating the cookies that were paired with the lemonade.

Z - "No, it's not that bloodline. It's the bloodline that created me," Zalena said. "Li-Chun and Dante must go back in a Time Portal and retrieve I.G.L.A. technology, and once that happens, we can move onto the next one," Zalena said.

Li-Chun couldn't believe Zalena, so she didn't speak. She just looked her up and down, studying her face. She walked around Zalena and checked her ankle for a birthmark. It was in the same location as her birthmark. Li-Chun went back around and hugged Zalena, before giving her a light smack across her cheek.

LC - "Don't put your family in stupid situations just because you want some action. We have enough problems. You do resemble Dante. I can't believe I didn't see that," Li-Chun scolded.

Z - "I'm sorry, Mother," Zalena said. She was the same age as her parents.

Scene 50 (Captain, My Captain)

{In orbit around Sirux-B, onboard *Curiosity*?}

Mary was floating around in her room. She was now looking at a hologram of Sirux-B and its moons, especially Zerux, which was the birthplace of the Zenon creatures. She couldn't find any readings indicating that a nearby Starship or source of energy was responsible for the radio wave takeover. She then went back over her data and io on the Zenon creatures that reminded her of upright walking lobsters.

She found it interesting that they communicated sending faint radio waves, using the electric current that their bodies produced inside of their shells. She thought it was an important thing to know. Because if that's how they communicate, then intercepting their natural signal could lead to her hijacking them. She felt as if she was making good progress, so she stopped and took a break.

They've been onboard the Pod *Curiosity* for at least one month. Mary found a way to make the walls in her living quarters simulate a sunset on her Earth. She also had the stars and moon appear on the ceiling when it was time to sleep. She loved that her brain could power majority of the ship's functions, as well as her suit. Her thoughts could make things appear such as Portals and Terminal. Dante's Terminal was manual, so he had to use his hand and fingers to operate it.

Mary thought she was just dreaming when she kept having visions involving Li-Chun and Dante in a church. She did the best she could to remember everything in her dream-like state. She sat straight up, no longer asleep, but fully conscience to her surroundings.

Mary sent Titan a message, via Thought Chip. They met up in the cockpit of *Curiosity* and sat in their chairs. Since Mary was the captain of her Pod, she could call the occupants to a meeting whenever she pleased.

> T - "So, what is the occasion for this call? Have you worked your magic yet?" Titan asked. "Not that I believe in that."

> M - "I wouldn't call it magic. More like investigation, but nevertheless, I think I have something," Mary said. "Okay,

the Zenon are being controlled by the small electric signals they produce to communicate with each other. I believe something is using them to rid the planet of the Reux. They emit a gas that directly impacts the atmosphere," Mary said, looking at a notepad she likes to carry onboard, as she sat in the seat wearing regular t-shirt and sweatpants.

T - "So, you think they are trying to terraform the planet?" Titan asked. "Maybe the atmosphere is the only thing stopping them from taking over the planet completely," Titan speculated.

M - "Yes, exactly. Since both of us are the products of another species creating us, the idea of letting any creature go extinct is not up for debate. So, let's suit, put our Exo-suits on. I want to return back to the surface of Sirux-B," Mary commanded.

T - "Confirmed Captain," Titan said, with his deep voice.

Scene 51 (Hunt for the Source of Corruption)

Mary and Titan were in their I.G.L.A. Spacesuits and Exo-suits, Mary was piloting *Curiosity* far above the planet. They were monitoring the moons and the planet for any signs of the Star Killers or their technology. She couldn't find the source. But kept checking her monitors that Titan shown her how to read.

M - "It's going to take some time, but I know I'm right Titan," Mary said. "We just have to be patient," Mary said.

T - "I think we should deploy our satellite, to scan the moons and go back to the surface of Sirux-B," Titan suggested.

M - "Okay. That sounds good. Let's go to the Safe Landing Zone for Sirux-B," Mary said, piloting the Pod.

T - "Since this will be our first time interacting with a hostile species you should activate your suit's Self-Defense Mode, which has more than one Mode. Select lethal, it creates a Force Field that uses Dark Matter and if touched, will send your aggressor to an alternate Dimension. You can also shoot charged Dark Matter, which moves at the speed of light and dissolves the enemy.

M - "Damn, that's cool. I hope I don't have to use any of that. But it's nice to have, since the Zenon spit acid," Mary said.

The Pod landed closer to the planet and the two went to the Lobby of the Pod and teleported to the surface of Sirux-B. The planet has a dense atmosphere and gravity that keeps them from floating around.

Mary and Titan activated the Anti-Gravity function on their suits and flown around like super-heroes, until they came across the Great Red Lakes. They floated above the surface of the Great Red Lakes, which were made of bubbling acid. The purple sky, red clouds, Great Red Lakes, and black vegetation was so beautiful Mary asked Titan if it were possible to take pictures of the scenery. He told her that she could, by thinking of the Camera Function and it would bring up options displayed in her Helmet Display Interface, which could be manipulated by her Thought Terminal Chip.

The Zenon lived in the acid lakes and fed on the black grass that grew everywhere. Staying well above the surface, looking like comic book heroes who could fly, they scanned the Zenon as they emerged from the red acid lake to feed on the black grass. Just then they got a reading from their deployable satellite, and it was from the water covered Zerux moon.

The satellite shown a spherical bubble that floated atop of the liquid water. The satellite gave a live-stream of footage and data that gave them a breakdown and analysis of the object. A bubble containing oxygen. The bubble was about the size of a house and was made of a transparent material, unknown to the Terminal Database. Titan cloaked the satellite and made it stop moving.

T - "We need to get back to the Pod now, Captain," Titan said. "We can end this now and return to the I.G.L.A. Starship."

Scene 52 (Is Its Wrong When We Do It?)

Titan and Mary used a Portal to get back to the Pod *Curiosity*. Mary was nervous, because all of the aliens she encountered thus far have been friendly up until this point. The idea of a murderous alien kind of shook her up, as they went through the Portal to travel back to the Ship.

They went back to the cockpit after removing their Exo-suits. Traveling to the moon's surface using incredible speed and Portal hopping, which let them travel extreme distances in a hurry. Once they arrived at the surface, they remained in the Pod. Titan touched the Pod's steering surface; it has a manual steering mechanism. He touched the screen with one of his big hairy fingers.

> T - "I'm going to send a message and you're the captain, so you get the task of making the Star Killers stop or face destruction," Titan said, calmly. "Time is important in this; they will use any chance to study us."

> M- "What? We give them a warning before we destroy their bubble pod thing. That's kind of strong of a reaction. Wouldn't that make us the Star Killers like them?" Mary asked, philosophically walking a tightrope.

> T - "I wouldn't say we are like them by destroying them for Genocide against vulnerable lifeforms. You can't let your guard down against Star Killers, they are highly intelligent beings and are only known for one thing and that's destruction. We have saved many countless planets and solar systems from them," Titan warned.

Mary then remembered that Titan and the Big Jellies' planets were destroyed by Star Killers. So, she understood why he had those feelings. Even though Titan was an oversized gorilla, he reminded her of a prideful man.

Mary typed an electric message on her Terminal. She wanted them to leave the solar system that Sirux-B was located in and to make themselves visible in their bubble. Also, explain why they are purposefully destroying the atmosphere and the intelligent beings that hold planetary knowledge, which creates more life in the long run.

The spherical object, the size of a home seemed to slowly become transparent. Mary and Titan were stunned at what they were looking at in the Bubble, floating above the endless ocean.

M - "Don't shoot anything at them. Stand down, Titan. That's an order," Mary said, cautiously.

Titan quickly removed his finger from the monitor that was showing a crosshair and all of their offensive weapons. They had multiple options which used some of their energy supply.

T- "Are you sure, Captain Mary?" Titan asked.

M - "I can't believe this s***!" Mary exclaimed, looking at the screen.

Scene 53 (Say Word)

{Zalena, Dante, Rebeccah, Li-Chun and Fatman. Earth's Core}

Everyone was sitting in the garden area, trying to grasp the concept of extra-dimension time travel. The team just learned about the Portal that led to the Time Portal, which allowed the two of them to go back in "Time" to prevent an ancient person from using the artifact and altering the Earth's history.

They also found out that Zalena was the daughter of Dante and Li-Chun. Beccah loved the dramatic aspect that ensued. She was loving every moment of the sci-fi drama. Zalena then accessed another Portal from her Terminal and this Portal was instead an old wooden Victorian-age door, that was standing upright with no frame or support, just like the previous one. Everyone went to quickly to look behind the door in disbelief. Nothing was behind it. Just a door in the colorful greenhouse area.

> R - "This is just like that scene from Monsters Inc, that door exists in another dimension. Wow, I never thought this was a real thing," Beccah explained.

> Z - "Exactly, Aunt," Zalena said. "Or should I just call you Rebeccah. I know it's weird since I'm older than you, old enough to be your big sister."

> R - "Beccah is just fine, Aunt makes me feel cringe. Now what happens when they open that door?" Beccah asked.

> Z - "We will just have to see, Beccah," Zalena said.

Li-Chun and Dante walked towards to the door. Dante stopped to give Beccah and Fatman a message.

> D - "Fatman and Beccah. Make sure you two keep each other safe, Li-Chun and I will make it back in one piece, I promise," Dante said, that made Beccah hug Dante, whom she looked up to.

She hugged Li-Chun, too, and Dante smiled. He knew why Beccah was so adamant that the two of them date. Somewhere down the line, they would eventually get married and have children, one that would travel back in time from the future to save Earth.

> R - "Say word. I should be telling you and Li-Chun that, but I gotcha, brother. I will protect my big homie and my big niece, sir," Rebeccah said, saluting him.

Dante looked at Beccah and exhaled, then nodded and opened the door and everyone just saw the blackness of the Portal. But once a nervous Dante and Li-Chun walked through the door, they were in an all-white interior and seemed to be walking on nothing. It was different than the few times they went through an actual Portal, which was quick and dark. This Portal was bright white with no actual floor, ceiling, or walls.

A door appeared in the distance, and it was an ancient and battered one. Dante recognized the language on the door: Hebrew. He hoped it wasn't going to be what he thought it was going to be once they walked through the Time Portal.

Scene 54 (Jesus Christ)

Li-Chun instantly recognized the way the buildings were made out of a brownish color and the way the people in the distance were dressed, that they were in the Ancient Middle East. She hoped they saw a Korean woman before, especially a tall one, one just as tall as Dante. They stood out in her mind.

They quickly walked to a field to get their bearings. Dante had a scarf on, which he quickly took off. He carefully wrapped it around her head and some of her face. Dante was a medium built man, muscle mass wise. He was in shape and very strong, because of his military training and being a gun-happy violent criminal. He had a big Bowie knife strapped on his thigh and was relieved. They both had on traditional garb of the time period. They checked their bodies for additional items placed on them to aid them in their mission.

LC - "Where are we, exactly?" Li-Chun asked. "I overheard some men speaking Hebrew. We are in the past, right? Look how we are dressed," Li-Chun pointed out.

D - "I believe this is Jerusalem. I can speak Hebrew fluently, so I'll translate it into sign language. I want you to be off the radar. This isn't our time in history where women are treated nicely. Let's not blow our cover because if we change what happens here, we will alter our modern time that we have to go back to. Let's not be characters in their history," Dante said, as he fashioned his scarf into a head covering for Li-Chun.

They went back to the town and Dante needed to find a place for them to stay for the night that was approaching. He asked Li-Chun to follow his lead, believing the people would be kind to travelers.

Dante and Li-Chun kept their heads down as they walked through the ancient Jerusalem city, full of different smells and sounds. A lot of the animals such as horses, donkeys, and goats were replacing the rats and dogs they were accustomed to. Li-Chun hated the animal smells.

The people had dark complexions and hairstyles that looked familiar to Dante, so it wouldn't be hard for him to blend in. Just then a man was running with a sack clutched in his arms. Another man emerged from his dwelling and shouted, "Stop! Thief!" Dante then gave chase to the man, quickly sprinting using his speed and tackled the man. Dante retrieved the sack and the man got up and ran away. He returned the sack back to the older man and he was thankful. He invited them both in and washed their feet.

I - "My name is Isaac, and this is my wife, Sarah. We are grateful that you stopped that thief with our grain. We would like to eat and have some drink with you and your wife. What's your name, my friends?" Isaac asked, being very hospitable.

D - "I'm Dante and my wife Li-Chun. We thank you a lot. But we need help," Dante requested. "We need a place to stay for the night, we've made a travel from a faraway land to get here," Dante said, Li-Chun following his lead and kept quiet.

S - "Sure, it'll be our honor, travelers. We will welcome you to our homeland properly," Sarah said, preparing their small, modest dinner table. "We open our home up to you."

Scene 55 (Human Star Killers)

{Onboard Astro-Pod *Curiosity*. Above the moon Zerux's Ocean Surface}

> M - "Human Star Killers? I can't believe this. We need to get
> a message from them," Mary said. "They can't see us, so they
> probably can't know if we we're friend or foe, I should—"

Mary was caught off by an incoming signal. As the Humans in the air bubble continued to float over the vast ocean, they had on skin tight gray suits and were sitting lotus style, floating inside of the bubble. The leader in the center was a middle-aged Black man, with a big Afro and a charming smile on his face.

> ? - "Hello. I'm just a guy trying to find a nice home for my
> family, that's all-space police," the mysterious man said on
> the signal.

Mary got up and went to into her Exo-suit, and Titan warned her to not do it. If she wanted to, she could send a Hologram-like version of herself that looked like her and even gave off a thermal signature. So, she quickly sat back down and accessed the huge screen in front of her. They had the window portion closed to hide themselves, so they could fake the Star Killers out.

Titan also cloned the Pod and moved their Pod; in case it was too close to the Star Killers. They watched from the eyes of the Hologram Clone of herself. The Pod was armed and in position to shoot its Dark Matter Projectiles that moved at the speed of light. The two watched on, as the man who was at the center of the translucent sphere floated lotus style to the edge to get a closer look at her Hologram, as it approached.

> ? - "I can tell you are Human come closer. What is your
> name? You look familiar," the man asked.

Mary's hologram drifted closer, and she was looking directly in the man's eyes, which were calming to her, as she hasn't seen another Human in a while. Mary was inside of the Pod, glued to the screen. Titan looked at her, not liking none of it.

M - "Yes. I am a Human, from the Earth that exists in this current Dimension. My name is Mary. I'm from the Intergalactic Liaison Allegiance. Our goal is to stop entities from destroying innocent life, you are in violation of planetary Genocide. You will cease your actions, now," Mary commanded, via signals on their frequency.

? - "You do know that there are no laws in deep space. You are very far from Earth at the moment young lady," the man said. "Would you kill another Human being in space for your masters? Humanity is violent, no matter what planet you're on. You're threatening our lives all the way out here, you're a hypocrite."

Her Hologram was looking serious as Mary herself was open mouthed in the Pod. Titan looked at her and the man.

T - "Captain. Do not fall for its tricks. These Star Killers sometimes disguise themselves by playing tricks with your mind and perception of reality," Titan warned.

M - "No. My dear Titan. I really believe he is a Human. We have to find a way to end this without violence. I want them detained. Humans in space is something I have to wrap my head around," Mary said, very intrigued by the situation.

Scene 56 (Walking on Water)

Li-Chun and Dante were asleep on a bed of straw, with a few hand-sewn blankets and were actually comfortable in Isaac and Sarah's home. The home was modest, but had art. Including sculptures, a drawing and a lot of scrolls. Dante and Li-Chun used sign language to communicate with each other. Dante couldn't take off his Terminal Watch. But it could cloak itself and disguise itself, which he loved.

> LC-We have a child together. How cool is that? I mean it does seem crazy right now. We are traveling through multi-dimensional Portals, through time and space and across the globe in our own Dimension," Li-Chun said. "I have your child and she traveled back in time to seek," Li-Chun signaled with her hands, smiling as she lay.

> D – "I'm sorry, I'm just bad at romance, but I've traveled back in time with you. And only we could go through that Portal, so that's Destiny calling," Dante said, signing back and mouthing his words. "I promise I enjoy being around you, that's why this is our mission and Zalena does look like us."

She quickly kissed him and kept quiet, out of respect for their hosts, who were not asleep that late night. Dante and Li-Chun faked their sleep sounds to eavesdrop on the couple to get a lay of the land. They were talking about the Messiah and how he was coming back to the town to preach and to meet up with his disciples. Sara ended the conversation, yawning deeply as they then went to bed.

They all woke up that morning all to wash their faces and hands before they broke bread and went on their own ways.

Dante and Li-Chun headed towards all the people who were gawking and talking loudly in the town's center, which was something they were used to in the Red-Light District Metropolis. But still kept their heads down, as they moved through the crowd to the cause of the hysteria.

They bore witness to the man Dante instantly recognized as Jesus. Dante found himself tearing up at the sight. Li-Chun looked over at him and didn't say anything. She was shocked, as well. They were witnessing the Black Jesus. How awesome it was to look at him. He had a medium-sized Afro and a big beard, but looked young and charming, as he had a very welcoming smile, riding on the back of a donkey.

D - "We have to track his moments and see where the artifact is that he has," Dante signed, in a low-key way for Li-Chun who was still in awe.

LC - "Yes, and remember, we can't interfere with what is going to happen to him. This is a covert, stealth mission. We can't save him. It will only result in an alternate reality in our timeline," Li-Chun said.

D - "I know. let's see how this plays out. Remember our time to fight will present itself," Dante said.

LC - "I can't wait. I love a good fight. Just like your daughter who sent tanks after her daddy and family," Li-Chun said, pinching his cheek.

Scene 57 (The Stargazers)

Mary and Titan were far away in the Pod. Three moons away from the ocean covered Zerux. They were still using the Hologram Pod and Hologram Mary. Mary started a weird and ethical space conversation, using her journalist skills to try to get information to slip from the mysterious man. She cut her off her mic, by tapping the screen on the cockpit dashboard, which she loved operating. She turned her gaze back to Titan.

M - "Titan, I think I should make a bold request. I think—"
Mary was cut off by Titan. Titan knew exactly what she was going to say.

T - "I should invite Hologram me inside of the Bubble." Titan tried his best to mock her light voice. His attempt made here giggle and her giggle made Titan chuckle, too.

M - "Okay. Let's try this before he gets suspicious," Mary said, turning her attention to the Star Killer. "I'm not trying to harm a fellow Human being. As a sign of good intentions, can I step inside of your bubble and talk to you?" she offered the man, looking at Titan in defiance.

? - "I'd like that. But you would have to come in person. I hate Holograms," the man said, smiling his welcoming smile.

M - "How did you know this is a Hologram? How is that possible?" Mary asked, confused.

? - "Come aboard the Bubble, and I'll tell you, "The man offered.

T - "Absolutely not. You can't just hop aboard a Star Killer Ship like that. This is too dangerous for you to do. Don't let a fellow species make you vulnerable and off-guard," Titan warned.

M - "I appreciate your support and advice. But back on Earth, I was around a lot of dangerous men and women. This is where I shine Titan, so please, back your captain up. Please, sir?" Mary said, using the same charm as the mysterious man.

T - "Yes, Captain. I'll be your support you. You Humans are very persuasive," Titan said.

M - "Okay. I'll do it. I'll just have to enter the Bubble in person," Mary said, talking back to mysterious man.

Titan and Mary ended the Hologram and Portal-hopped to the surface of Zerux. The real Mary exited the pod the manual way, through the main lobby.

T - "Remember, the terminal can't be taken off at all, unless you cut off your small hand," Titan advised.

She left the Pod, descending in her Exo-suit. In addition to her I.G.L.A. all-purpose Suit and Helmet, her main tools in her arsenal. She floated down through the atmosphere, towards the Bubble in her Exo-suit. The man politely stopped her. A small bubble that she could fit in appeared by her.

? - "Miss Mary, your Exo-suit and I.G.L.A, please. Spacesuits would disrupt our Bubble; you'd have to come in without it on. I don't want you naked though. You can wear simple cotton clothes in our Bubble. We know you wear them under your suit," the man instructed.

Scene 58 (Twenty-One Questions from Rebeccah)

{The Sanctuary, the Center of the Earth}

Zalena was playing host to Rebeccah and Fatman, who were bored, prompting Beccah to ask Zalena all sort of questions. They sat around in the pews of the vast sanctuary. They moved from the garden area back to the Gothic-looking underground Temple.

R#1 - "Exactly how old are you? You look extremely young to be so wise and smart?" Beccah asked, braiding her Afro using her pick which she always carried.

Z#1 - "To be honest. I don't know. I've stopped trying to keep track. Don't forget, I'm going to be born two years from now. But I come from the future. I travel back and forth in time and space," Zalena answered.

R#2 - "Okay, that's some futuristic kinda s***. Have you ever met yourself time traveling, and was it weird?" Rebeccah asked.

Z#2 - "I have seen myself quite a few times in a few different dimensions in the Multiverse. I've never interacted with myself though. I'd have to hide my identity to avoid not existing at all," Zalena answered.

R#3 - "How many aliens have you interacted with? Was it scary to you?" Beccah inquired. She was using both of her knees to hold a small mirror, braiding her own hair.

Z#3- "I've seen four different alien species. I fainted every time. Some people can handle it better than I can." Zalena smiled.

R#4 - "Where is my sister?" Rebeccah asked.

Z#4- "Your sister is with the Intergalactic Liaison Allegiance; I.G.L.A for short. I don't know exactly where she is. More than likely, she's on a distant planet or moon, doing whatever the I.G.L.A. says," Zalena said.

R#5 - "What is her job title?" Rebeccah asked.

Z#5 - "Her job title is going to be whatever her special skill is. In her case, being an investigative journalist," Zalena stated.

R#6 - "What kind of activities does the I.G.L.A. engage in and please tell me it's like *Star Wars*?" Beccah asked, getting excited.

Z#6 - "That's exactly what it is. Her first time onboard their planet-sized Starship is going to be crazy for her. I bet she has seen so many aliens, the next time you see her, she will look older as a result," Zalena said.

R#7 - "Have you had a romantic fling with any historical figure in your time-traveling adventures?" Beccah was wide eyed and loved Zalena's answers.

Z#7 - "Yes. I once dated Hannibal of Carthage and was a concubine of Cleopatra, who was sexier than the movies portray her to be," Zalena said, with a twinkle in her eye.

R#8 - "Okay, cool. Will Humanity ever solve man made climate change, or will we continue to destroy our Earth?" Rebeccah asked.

Z#8 - "I can't answer that, or it will interrupt the Time Paradox. Just as I can't interact with myself," Zalena answered.

R#9 - "How were the pyramids built? How did they move those huge blocks of stone?" Rebeccah asked, halfway through with her hair.

Z#9 - "They used water to float the huge stones. True masters of water irrigation," Zalena said.

R#10 - "You're blowing my mind right now, Unc, are you hearing this?" Beccah asked, punching his arm. "Did we go to Mars in my lifetime?" Beccah continuing her line of questions.

Z#10 - "If I tell you this, you have to keep it a secret," Zalena warned, extending her pinky. Beccah hooked it with her small pinky. "Aunt Rebeccah. Yes. A very bold man funded a five-year, multi-trillion-dollar trip to the Red Planet and back. To return to Earth, they had to catch the Earth in a certain orbit," Zalena described.

R#11 - "If the planet is truly under the watch of advanced beings, then what do they think of our trip to Mars?" Rebeccah asked.

Z#11 - "That I don't know, I try not to be around them long, it's scary," Zalena said.

R#12 – "Why do you like being in the center of the Earth? Don't the Mercury Order own above ground property?" Beccah asked.

Z#12 - "The Mercury Order does indeed have an above ground sanctuary. Luckily, my assignment landed me here. I love being here. After we get the three artifacts, I will be back in my timeline."

R#13 - "Will any of us die on this journey we're on?" Beccah asked.

Z#13 - "I don't know, I hope not," Zalena answered, honestly.

R#14 - "How many planets did my Earthlings walk on?" Beccah asked.

Z#14 - "People from you're Earth reached two planets in your lifetime. Many died along the way. But it was accomplished," Zalena stated.

R#15 - "We're those two trips assisted by E.T.s at all?" Rebeccah asked.

Z#15 - "No, all Human effort," Zalena answered, simply.

R#16 - "Do you want a romantic interest?" Beccah asked.

Z#16 - "Yes. After this I'm going to date a normal guy and chill all the way out." Zalena grinned, broadly and proudly.

R#17 - "What kind of guys do you like?" Beccah asked, almost finished with her hair.

Z#17 - "Straightforward and believe in something," Zalena simply said.

R#18 - "Anybody throughout history that loved Black culture I wouldn't know about?" Beccah asked.

Z#18 - "Thomas Jefferson comes to my mind first." Zalena smirked.

R#19 - "Will Humanity defeat racism?" Rebeccah asked.

Z#19 – "Not in our lifetime. I haven't traveled that far back in time, Aunt B.," Zalena answered.

R#20/21 - "Will I go to Space? Will I ever see Sis again?" Rebeccah asked, afraid of both answers.

Z#20/21 - "Yes, to both, Aunt. And I will be by your side during both," Zalena said, trying to be comforting to her teenage aunt.

Scene 60 (Let the Prophecy Unravel)

(Jerusalem)

They all watched as the Messiah interact with his disciples, as they set out to preach. Dante heard a commotion and recognized the voices in distress. It was no other than Isaac and Sarah. They were being harassed by a big Roman soldier. Dante hated how they were off to the side in an isolated place, far away the crowd.

Dante and Li-Chun went to investigate. It looked like the Roman soldier wanted a fight that no one could see. He seemed to truly desire to hurt them. Dante was going to confront the soldier that had a small Stargaze Society tattoo.

> D - "We have to knock him out and tie him up. We could kill him, but I don't know how this Time Paradox s*** works yet," Dante said, still using sign language.

> LC - "I want to do it. It's been a while since my last action sequence in the book. I want to see how much stronger the author has made me. I may have developed plot armor," Li-Chun said.

> D - "What?" Dante asked quizzically. "This isn't some sci-fi fantasy drama. This is real, with real consequences," Dante warned.

Sarah stepped in front of Isaac to confront the soldier. He drew his sword on the woman. Dante and Li-Chun wanted to step forward but stopped once they saw the confident smile on Sarah's face. She stepped out of her sandals and lifted up her garments up to her knees. Holding them above her knees and squatting, showing her fighting stance. The soldier charged forward and swung the sword overhead, which made Sarah swiftly move to the side, making his sword strike the ground. She punched the big soldier in the face with a solid punch. The huge man ate the punch and swung the sword again. Sarah still held her dress with one hand and ducked, making the sword bury into the ground. The sword flew over her head, dust flying everywhere.

She used one hand to keep her balance as she kicked the soldier's leg from up under him. He fell on his back; his sword left his grip and flew in the air above him. Sarah hopped back up quickly and grabbed his sword before it plunged in his chest. He smiled knowing she wouldn't kill him. Sarah instead used her barefoot to kick his face and knockout him out. She and Isaac moved his body to not be found. Sarah dusted herself off after kicking the soldier's a**.

Dante and Li-Chun went back into the crowd by the marketplace, where people sold their goods and services. They found the Messiah and his disciples by a blind man, who wanted to be healed. Dante watched as the Messiah and his disciples preached and touched the man. His gray eyes became brown and full of curiosity, as the man hugged the Messiah. He joked about his beggar friends looks, as it was his first time seeing them.

Later, after the miracle, a soldier came and confronted Jesus and his disciples. They flanked them, seeing them as a threat. Jesus didn't get nervous. He greeted them and even bowed, as the soldier came in his face, sneering.

> RS - "It's the Messiah, he King of all kings. You deceive the people, this time healing the blind beggar," the Roman official said.

> J - "I deceive none. I only teach the way of my Heavenly Father. I'm his instrument for love and peace, for all men," Jesus said.

> RS - "I will end this when the time permits me to, Messiah," the Roman soldier boasted.

Scene 61 (It's Gonna Be Alright)

{The Sanctuary, Earth's Core}

Zalena, Rebeccah, and Fatman were sparring and shadowboxing. Beccah wanted to fight the taller and quicker Zalena. Beccah was sweaty as she stopped to take a breath and drink some water from a big wine glass. Zalena had her own dishes in the sanctuary, which she treated like an apartment. A T.V. and game console were powered by her Terminal, which had an unlimited power source and could power any electronic device.

Rebeccah resumed her sparring session with Zalena. Beccah was studying Zalena. She noticed Zalena moved similarly to her mother Li-Chun, who was taller and a lot stronger. Zalena was a very young woman, whose face appeared a few years older because of her ability to travel in time and access the Multiverse, which causes stress. Zalena caught herself thinking of her parents and their survival, when she suddenly felt her feet give way, making her fall backwards. Fatman caught her as he watched them both spar, taking their frustrations out on each other.

> R - "I can't fight a distracted sparring partner; let's take a break and talk, Zalena," Rebeccah said, placing her hand on Zalena's arm.

They went to the T.V. and sat down on some pillows that decorated a Gothic-style pew in the sanctuary. Deep in the molten core of the planet. Zalena sighed as she watched *SpongeBob*. Beccah loved the show, too. It calmed them both down, like little kids. Fatman was babysitting. He saw that their emotional guard was being let down by the show, so he made a therapy session out of it.

> F - "What's on your mind, Zalena? You can tell us anything. I mean we are family. Is it your parents?" Fatman asked.

> Z - "Yeah. I'm worried about them, I mean…" Zalena exhaled deeply. "You think they are alright. I can't stop thinking about them," Zalena asked.

F - "Of course. They are fine," Fatman said, softly and calmly. "Don't forget, you did chase us with a tank; it was Dante who led us to safety and Li-Chun who saved him from the assassins and the police commissioner. So, they are fine," Fatman said. They both smiled.

Z - "Yeah. But that was B.S. I wasn't going to kill you guys, I just wanted to see if the legend was true, and it definitely is. But I have a question?" Zalena asked. "What are they really like? Why are the two of them so serious?" Zalena asked.

R - "Well, my brother is a really serious dude, his soft spot is his family and Li-Chun," Rebeccah answered. "Li-Chun is a woman who sacrifices for the benefit of others."

Z - "How did they meet? How can someone so ruthless and brutal be so shy towards a nice woman like Li-Chun?" Zalena asked.

F - "Well, we were in a dangerous business, and we only were brutal towards criminals and drug dealers. We never hurt any civilians," Fatman said. "Li-Chun is kinda intimidating, you can't blame him. And he can't be that shy if you exist."

R - "Li-Chun is his kryptonite. She comes from a hard working family but navigates the rough life Dante and you live. They met in high school and I could tell growing up that they both liked each other. Recently, I made them go out on a date and they announced they are going to date. So, your existence may well be contributed to me. Thank you."

Scene 62 (The Big Reveal)

{The Bubble, Above Zerux's Ocean Covered Surface}

The mysterious man used a wave of the hand and a smaller bubble separated itself from the bigger bubble. Mary was calm as the bubble floated towards her above the surface of the ocean-covered moon. She was in her Exo-suit and normal I.G.L.A. suit that protected her from radiation and dangerous atmospheric pressures that she faces on strange planets and moons.

She entered the bubble and her Exo-suit scanned the bubble to see if it was safe to be inside, without the protection of her suit. Once it said the oxygen level and atmospheric pressure was stable to be in without any suit, she started the process of taking off her clothes. She took off both suits and they both went into their compact forms. Mary only had on a sports bra and shorts as she floated in the smaller bubble alongside the bigger one.

There were three men and three women, plus the pilot, who was black and had a big beard. They all wore skin tight gray jump suits and had the Stargaze logo on their chest. Seeing that logo confused her, as she sat Lotus style like them.

> ? - "Greetings, I am—" the Mysterious man said, before stopping. "I'll let you figure that part out as we go on."

Mary looked at the other humans who were paying attention but were quiet. One woman smiled warmly, after looking at Mary's terminal and they all noticed her.

> M - "I'm here on behalf of the innocent Reux, that you are killing with your actions on this moon," Mary said, going all business. "They may not mean anything to you. But they are very old organisms and have knowledge on Humans, we could learn a lot from not destroying their home."

{The Bubble}

> ? - "I can tell that you are new to your job, but that's fine. I get it, I totally get it. You're young, naive, and brave. Trying

to please your boss," the bearded mystery man said, speaking softly.

M - "You don't know me at all. Don't speak on me like that and before you say anything, I know how this talk is going to go. I know you're going to say that," Mary said, before being cut off.

? - "I'm your father," the man interjected.

M - "What? I wasn't going to go that far," Mary said, she was confused. "So, all this time we were looking for our father, you were up here? Playing God in Space," Mary said, getting mad.

? - "The story is deeper than that. I will gladly explain if you don't kill us," the bearded man pleaded.

M - "I wouldn't kill you in cold-blood. But I'm going to have to arrest you on charges of planetary Genocide against an innocent species. We can talk before I detain all of you," Mary said.

? - "Wow, arresting your father? That's bold of you. That comes from your mother. Don't you find it strange, that your first mission for the I.G.L.A. would result in finding your biological father. Then arresting him on the charges of genocide?" the man asked.

M - "Okay, let's talk then. I want to hear your side of the story," Mary said.

To be Continued in BLACKSPACE:
Book 2, Vengeance.
Buckle up for the conclusion.

www.ingramcontent.com/pod-product-compliance
Lightning Source LLC
Chambersburg PA
CBHW071322150726
47997CB00002B/570